"I'm as fat as a sow. I know. And just as ugly."

Her lower lip jutted out now in a full-fledged pout. "How unchivalrous of you to point that out."

"Oh, no, *querida*." His hands moved to cup her face, and the grin he'd been sporting was replaced by an expression of such earnest warmth that it fairly melted Emily's heart. "A woman can never look ugly when she is brimming with life."

Emily couldn't break her gaze from those incredibly warm eyes. She didn't want to. All of a sudden, instead of feeling like an awkward, overgrown sow, she felt like a swan, all featherlight and full of grace.

"Go," he said. "Before I kiss you." He angled his head toward the door of the saloon.

Suddenly Emily couldn't think of anything in the world she wanted more than for John to kiss her....

Dear Reader,

Much of the beauty of romance novels is that most are written by women for women, and feature strong and passionate heroines. We have some stellar authors this month who bring to life those intrepid women we love as they engage in relationships with the men we also love!

Mary McBride's poetic voice and powerful stories have won her numerous historical romance fans. And with the recent debut of her first contemporary romance from Silhouette, Mary's audience keeps expanding. *Bandera's Bride* is a heartwarming Western about two misfits who fall in love through letters. But when Southern belle Emily Russell, now pregnant, decides to travel to Texas to propose marriage to her letter lover, she finds only his half-breed partner, John Bandera. Neither dreams of achieving the other's love—only they magically do.

Susan Amarillas brings us a new Western, *Molly's Hero,* a tale of forbidden love between a—married?—female rancher and the handsome railroad builder who desperately needs her land. In *The Viking's Heart,* a medieval novel by rising talent Jacqueline Navin, Rosamund Clavier is the proud noblewoman who falls in love with the fierce Viking sent to escort her to her own arranged marriage. Will she choose love or duty?

And don't miss *My Lady's Dare,* by the sensational Gayle Wilson. This Regency-set tale will grab you and not let go as the Earl of Dare becomes fascinated by another man's mistress. Nothing is as it seems in this dangerous game of espionage and love!

Enjoy! And come back again next month for four more choices of the best in historical romance.

Sincerely,

Tracy Farrell,
Senior Editor

MARY McBRIDE

BANDERA'S BRIDE

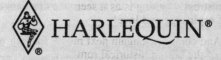

HARLEQUIN®

TORONTO • NEW YORK • LONDON
AMSTERDAM • PARIS • SYDNEY • HAMBURG
STOCKHOLM • ATHENS • TOKYO • MILAN • MADRID
PRAGUE • WARSAW • BUDAPEST • AUCKLAND

ISBN 0-373-29117-5

BANDERA'S BRIDE

This edition published by arrangement with Harlequin Books S.A.

® and TM are trademarks of the publisher. Trademarks indicated with
® are registered in the United States Patent and Trademark Office, the
Canadian Trade Marks Office and in other countries.

Visit us at www.eHarlequin.com

Printed in U.S.A.

Available from Harlequin Historicals and
MARY McBRIDE

Other works include:

Harlequin Books

Silhouette Intimate Moments

Please address questions and book requests to:
Harlequin Reader Service
U.S.: 3010 Walden Ave., P.O. Box 1325, Buffalo, NY 14269
Canadian: P.O. Box 609, Fort Erie, Ont. L2A 5X3

For the men in my life—Leslie, Loren and Merit

Prologue

Texas, 1866

It wasn't a perfect partnership, the one between the Southerner, Price McDaniel, and the half-breed, John Bandera. It was as far from perfect as the rugged landscape of south Texas was from the gentle hills of Russell County, Mississippi. The two men had almost nothing in common.

Physically, they were as mismatched as daylight and dark. McDaniel was a slight man with hair as fair as corn silk. John Bandera, the dark half of the equation, had bronze skin and cast-iron black hair. Part Comanche, part Mexican, and part anybody's guess, he was imposing in size alone, but it was his amber, catlike gaze that kept most men at a wary distance. His partner, Price McDaniel, was usually too drunk to be cautious.

When drunk, which was often, Price was a man given to lengthy proclamations uttered in a drawl that was one third Mississippi and the rest pure Tennessee whiskey. John Bandera rarely drank and said little in return.

The two men didn't even particularly like each other. Still, they were partners, bound by a single and uncharacteristic burst of heroism at the Cimarron Crossing in 1864 when Lieutenant McDaniel had saved Scout Bandera's life.

Despite their differences, the partnership—thus far—had proven beneficial for both of them. The year before, after being mustered out of the army, Price had had more money than good sense, and he had wanted to build a ranch in Texas to rival anything back in Russell County, Mississippi, no matter that he didn't know a longhorn from a mule deer or a heifer from a steer.

John had been broke, physically as well as financially. The army had no use for a scout on crutches and John had needed a place to heal. He'd owed Price for saving his life, and he figured one year of his sweat and expertise would cancel his debt to the Southerner.

Now that year was up.

The house was finally finished. Its pine floors and door frames glowed a rich gold beneath a first coating of shellac. The place still smelled of sawdust, but that raw odor mingled now with the fragrance of oiled walnut and rich leather.

Price McDaniel's furniture—two wagon loads all the way from Mississippi—had arrived earlier in the day. There were wardrobes, chairs and sofas, dressers, mirrors, all manner of beds and bedding. There was one big swivel chair that matched one enormous desk. And there had also been one cream-colored letter tucked neatly inside the center drawer.

Price had been on a tear ever since finding it. He had read the letter at least a dozen times, and had looked at the enclosed *carte de visite* long enough and hard enough to wear the chemicals right off the little photograph. At the moment, the picture lay facedown on the desktop, the envelope was strewn in little pieces on the floor, and Price was fashioning the letter itself into a rough approximation of a bird.

"Ladies," he slurred as he folded one edge of the vellum, then crimped it, "especially those of the Southern persuasion, are like gardenias. Have you ever seen a gardenia, John?"

As lamplight glanced off the fresh pine paneling, it made the half-breed's eyes all the more amber when he looked up from the list of supplies he was composing—goods intended to see his soon-to-be ex-partner through the coming winter.

"Nope," he replied, about to add that he'd

never seen a lady, either. Instead he returned his attention to his list, knowing Price would go on with his drunken declamation whether anyone was listening or not.

He did, interspersing his words with wet, laborious sighs.

"They're all pale and creamy and petal-soft. Dewy and cool to the touch. Only you can't. Touch them, I mean. Southern ladies are just for the looking. Touch them, and they bruise. Just like a gardenia. You remember that, John, if you ever have the supreme misfortune to meet up with one of them."

"I'll keep it in mind." His chances of meeting up with a lady, Southern or otherwise, were slim, slimmer, and none, John thought. The notion that he'd ever have the opportunity to touch one struck him as ludicrous. He'd learned early and at the painful end of a switch not to want what he couldn't have. Ladies were high on that particular list.

He made a last notation now on his own list, then parked the pencil stub behind his ear. "If you're all done ranting, Price, maybe we could go over a few things."

The Mississippian smiled sloppily as he lifted the folded letter, held it shoulder-high a second, then launched it across the room. The pale paper flew like a snub-nosed, stubby-winged owl before it plummeted to the floor beside John's moccasined foot.

He ignored it a moment, then picked it up and smoothed it out across his knee, instantly intrigued by the daintiness of the penmanship, trying to imagine the pale, fine-boned fingers that had drafted each delicate word.

He read not the whole, but separate, beautifully crafted words and phrases here and there. *How delighted we all were. Sympathetic to your dire circumstances as a prisoner of war. Russell County. Do remember. Forever your home.*

His amber eyes flicked up to meet his partner's. "You going back?"

Price chuckled softly as he filled his empty glass from the bottle near his elbow, then raised the glass in a wavering salute.

"Here's to Russell County, Mississippi, where a Russell is always a Russell and everybody else is…everybody else."

He downed half the whiskey, then continued. "And here's to Miss Emily Russell. May she bloom and prosper in Russell County soil. Here's to gardenias in all their pale and untouchable glory."

Price drained his glass and thumped it down on the desktop. "Here's to us, partner. And to the frigid day in hell that finds me back in Mississippi."

"You're staying." It wasn't a question so much as an acknowledgment. A disappointed one. John had hoped for a moment that Price would go home. It was where the man belonged, after all. So what if he had turned his back on the Confederacy in order to get out of a Yankee prison? He hadn't been the only Rebel prisoner who'd put on a blue uniform and headed west as a Galvanized Yankee.

But he didn't belong out West anymore. He belonged back home with well-bred gentlemen like himself and with ladies like gardenias. And he was damned lucky, in John's estimation, to have a place where he belonged.

"I'm staying." Price's clenched fists banged hard on the desktop. "Russell County be damned, along with all the Russells in it." He picked up the little *carte de visite* and, without even glancing at it, flicked it across the desk toward John. "Good riddance to them all."

John's dark hand shot out to catch the photograph before it fluttered to the floor. It felt warm in his palm, almost alive. He stared at its blank side a moment, as if hesitant to look at the face of the woman…no, the lady…whose delicate hand had composed the letter still lying on his leg. What face could be flawless enough? What pose perfect enough? What tilt of chin or hint of smile could be worthy of the lady in his head?

This one! His heart bunched up in his throat

when he gazed at Emily Russell, and as his sun-bronzed thumb smoothed over the photograph, he wouldn't have been at all surprised to see her lovely image begin to wither and fade. What was it Price had said? *Touch them, and they bruise.*

John had to clear his throat before he spoke, but there was still an unfamiliar, nearly ragged catch.

"She's a lady, Price. You ought to write her back."

"Like hell," his partner snorted, replenishing his glass, sloshing whiskey over the rim. "Since when are you so concerned with proprieties?"

Since a minute ago, John wanted to say, but he merely shook his head and muttered, "It's the right thing to do."

Price rolled his eyes. "Well, you go on and write her, then, if you feel so strongly about it. Go on, John. Be my guest. Write the lady back."

He did. Then, although he'd meant to leave when that first year was up, John Bandera hung around waiting for a reply.

When it came—addressed to Price—he wrote her back.

And waited again. And again.

Six years later, long after his drunken partner had pulled up stakes and disappeared, John Bandera was still there, still writing letters signed "Price," still loving the lady so like a gardenia.

Chapter One

Mississippi, 1872

"Emily Russell, you are not leaving. I forbid it. Now, you put that suitcase down. Do you hear me? Put it down."

"I do hear you, Dodie. You're screeching like an owl, and I wouldn't be a bit surprised if everybody in Russell County hears you."

"You wouldn't be doing this if your brother were here. After all Elliot's done for you, too. How can you be such an ungrateful wretch?"

Emily shoved past her wailing sister-in-law, charged through the front door, and dropped her final piece of luggage on the verandah.

"There." She shaded her eyes against the bright morning sun, searching past the long sweep of driveway toward the street beyond. "Now, where in blazes is Haley Gates? He promised me he'd be here by ten o'clock.''

"If I know Haley Gates," Dodie muttered, "he's probably facedown in the hay in somebody's barn." Then she reached for the leather handle of a carpetbag. "I'm taking this back inside."

Emily jerked the bag away. "You'll do no such thing. I'm going, Dodie. And that's that."

"To Texas!" The young woman threw up her hands. "Texas! Where you'll be set upon by wild Indians. Maybe even scalped. Lord knows any savage would love to whack off those blond curls of yours."

"I'll be sure and keep my bonnet tied tight, then." Emily peered down the street in the opposite direction. "I'll scalp that Haley if he's not here in two more minutes."

Dodie sighed mightily, then sank into a high-backed wicker chair. "Elliot's going to be beside himself when he gets back from New Orleans to find you've taken off like some thief in the night. You know that, don't you? He'll be furious. He feels so responsible for you."

"It's ten o'clock in the morning, Dodie, and I'm not a thief. I'm not a prisoner, either. At least not anymore."

"A prisoner! What a spiteful thing to say, Emily, when all we've done is look out for your best interests since Mother and Father Russell passed away. Why, I'm sure those two must be fairly twirling in their graves right now, seeing what their foolish, dreamy daughter is up to.''

Emily almost laughed at that image of her prim and proper parents. But Dodie was probably right. If they knew what she was doing, her parents would most definitely spin in their shady little graves. As for being dreamy… Well, Dodie was probably right about that, too. But Emily wasn't foolish. Not now, at least.

Dodie sighed again, louder and longer. ''Oh, how I wish that nice Mr. Gibbons hadn't gotten the croup and died. He was going to propose marriage, Emily. After all those years of being so shy and tongue-tied whenever he was around you, I simply know he'd worked up the courage to pop the question. I could see it in his eyes.''

''Perhaps,'' Emily said. And she would have married Alvin Gibbons, too, she thought. She would have had to marry him, and then they would have lived unhappily ever after. Only now her longtime, flesh-and-blood suitor was dead and Emily was on her way to Texas to find a man she didn't know in the flesh, but in letters. All those lovely letters.

''I'd like to scalp that no-good Price McDaniel for luring you away like this,'' Dodie moaned.

''He didn't lure me.'' Emily almost laughed at her sister-in-law's melodramatic despair. If anybody deserved to be melodramatic and despairing right now, it was Emily herself. "Price doesn't even know I'm coming."

"Well, that's just fine and dandy. You're traveling five thousand miles to see a man—a traitor, by the way—who may or may not even be there when you arrive."

"It's not five thousand miles. And Price is not a traitor. He did what he had to do, Dodie, to get out of that horrible Yankee prison camp. You know that."

"He should have come home."

Emily gave an indignant snort. "To what sort of welcome?"

They had had this argument before, a hundred times perhaps during Emily's six-year correspondence with the self-exiled Price McDaniel. But what her sister-in-law failed to recognize was that, during those six years, Emily had fallen in love with the man. She hadn't told a soul, though.

Well, that wasn't quite true. She had confessed her love to Price in a ten-page, heartfelt letter she had written on New Year's Eve, then sealed and mailed with such high hopes on the first day of 1872.

If you think me bold and brazen, dearest Price, then I am guilty as charged. Your Emmy loves you and would even be so bold as to propose a life together in the flesh rather just on paper. Send for me, Price. Oh, my dearest. Marry me.

His response had arrived, like clockwork, as all his previous letters had, and she had opened it with a brimming heart and trembling hands only to read his bitterly fond and conclusive farewell.

Someday I hope you can forgive me for misleading you. Dearest Emmy, I will not write again.

That evening she had wept on Alvin Gibbons's shoulder, and he—suddenly not so shy—had consoled her gently, if not a bit too thoroughly, just two weeks before he sickened and died.

"For God's sake," Dodie exclaimed now. "You barely knew Price when he was here and you haven't heard a word from him in months. How do you know he's still in Texas? How do you know he's still alive? Or that he even wants to see you?"

"I know," Emily lied, when what she knew was only that she had to leave. Today. Now. It wouldn't be long before everyone in Russell County knew that she—poor Emily, the dreamy spinster, the maiden lady whose shy suitor had passed away three months ago—was going to have a child.

Haley Gates had a tendency to spit when he talked, in part from his habit of dipping snuff and in part from the absence of front teeth, so while Emily sat beside him on the wagon seat, she was glad he kept his face forward and his eyes on the backsides of his mules. She was glad, too, that he had lapsed into silence after an hour-long discourse on who was up to what in Russell County. The man took extraordinary pleasure in pawing through almost everybody's dirty laundry. Almost everybody. Her own secret, she supposed, was still safe.

But if he said one more time just how brave she was for going out West alone, Emily couldn't decide whether she was going to hit him or to ask him to turn the wagon around and take her home. She didn't feel brave. She felt sick and scared to death.

Even so, there was no going back. Her decision wasn't based so much on the scandal her family would have to endure or her own sorry future as a fallen woman, but on the pitiful prospects for a child born out of wedlock in an unforgiving community.

She glanced at the unfortunate man beside her. Haley Gates was nearly forty years old, but tongues still wagged about his illegitimate origin, and more people than not referred to him as Sally Gates's bastard boy.

That wouldn't happen to her child, by God. He or she was going to have a chance in this unforgiving world. Emily meant to see to that, no matter how sick or scared she felt. No matter how ashamed she felt for closing her eyes that night and pretending Alvin Gibbons was the man she loved, that his hands were Price McDaniel's hands, that his kisses were the ones she craved, and that he loved her as desperately as she loved him.

"...friends or kinfolk?"

With a jolt, Emily realized that Haley had been speaking to her and she hadn't comprehended a single word he'd said. She apologized.

"Oh, that's all right, Miss Emily. A mind tends to wander on a pretty day like this." He spat, this time intentionally, over the side of the wagon. "I was just asking who you planned on visiting in Texas. I didn't know any Russells had ever left the county."

"Only my uncle Randolph," she said. "And he went east to Washington, D.C."

"So you're visiting a friend, then?"

"Yes. A friend."

What did it matter now, telling Haley the truth? she wondered. Knowing Dodie's proclivity for gossip, she was certain the entire Ladies' Aid Society already knew her destination. And if the venerable LAS knew, then everybody in seven counties was sure to know within a week.

"I've been corresponding with Price Mc-Daniel," she said as matter-of-factly as she could. "He chose to stay out West after the war to raise cattle. And he's cordially invited me to visit his ranch."

Haley took one hand from the reins in order to scratch his head. "McDaniel. McDaniel. That doesn't strike any particular bell."

"Well, he's been gone for quite some time. He had no sisters or brothers, and his parents passed away several years ago. They lived in that big white house on Solomon Street."

"Oh, those McDaniels." Haley slapped his knee. "I remember them, all right. Why, I even helped tote all that furniture they shipped to Texas."

"Yes. I remember, too."

What Emily remembered was slipping an envelope into a drawer of an enormous walnut desk, and then a month later being surprised by a thoughtful reply, written in a bold and quite masculine hand. The tone of the letter had been serious and almost poetic, which surprised her even more, because her memory of Price had been that of a laughing and rather cavalier young man, given more to pranks than poetry.

How the war had changed him, she had thought

at the time, and then with each successive letter, she found herself increasingly glad that the callow youth she recalled had been forged into such a strong yet gentle man.

Then, month by month, letter by letter, Emily had fallen in love. It had been her distinct impression, even her devout belief, that Price's feelings for her were of an equal depth and weight. *Dear Miss Russell* had long ago been replaced by *Dear,* then *Dearest Emily.* The second to the last letter— the one to which she had responded with such candor and passion—had begun *My Dearest Emmy.*

That one—the one with half its inked words dripping down the pages from her happy tears— was now wrapped in a lace hanky and tucked deep inside the reticule on her lap. Price's other letters, tied with silk ribbons, a different color for every year, were secure in her leather valise. And although she had packed most of her clothes and other belongings for the trip to Texas, nothing really mattered but the letters that had come to be her most valuable possessions, indeed her only priceless worldly goods.

"All that furniture," Haley murmured, shaking his head. "I sure do remember now that you mention it, Miss Emily. Wonder if all them dressers and desks and whatnots made it to Texas all right. Did you ever hear?"

Emily smiled wistfully. "The desk arrived, Haley. That's all I know for sure."

The levee in Vicksburg was crowded when they arrived later that afternoon. Haley's mule-drawn wagon wasn't the worst-looking vehicle at the steamboat landing, but it didn't rank far above most of the produce wagons parked there. For one bleak moment, Emily felt that she had come down a peg or two in the world until she reminded herself of her fallen status and decided she was lucky indeed to even be able to afford a wagon ride, not to mention the passage she had booked on the *Memphis Zephyr*, whose smokestacks were already billowing with steam.

"I must hurry, Haley," she said, clambering down from the wagon seat before he could come to her aid, then reaching for the valise that held her precious letters. "If you'll carry my other bags to the gangplank, I'd be most appreciative."

Emily hurried across the cobblestones to show her ticket to the captain.

He squinted at her from beneath the polished brim of his cap. "You traveling alone, Miss Russell?"

After she nodded, the man handed her ticket back, then lightly touched her arm. "I'll keep a special eye out for you. Fine family, those people of yours. I've met your uncle, the legislator, on one or two occasions.''

"How nice," she replied while thinking that her uncle Randolph would likely be the first to disown her in light of her condition.

"You give him my regards when next you see him, will you?"

"Indeed I will, Captain."

"Is that your man with your luggage?" he asked, angling his head toward Haley, who was just then waging a losing battle with a small steamer trunk, a suitcase, and two carpetbags.

The captain gestured to one of his crewmen, a muscular man. "See that Miss Russell's luggage makes it to her stateroom, will you?"

Then, after the captain turned to greet other passengers, Emily walked back to bid farewell to Haley.

He stood, gazing forlornly at the ground, the worn toe of one boot lodged between two cobblestones.

"Well, I guess it's time for you to get on board," he said. Then he looked up and gave her a wide but toothless grin. "I kinda wish I was going with you, Miss Emily. Out West, you know. Where things is all brand-new."

"Brand-new," she echoed, despite the lump in her throat, suddenly feeling far sorrier for Haley than she did for herself. "Well, come along then," she said, surprising herself by how much she meant it. "Come west with me where things are indeed all brand-new."

Haley toed the cobblestones again. "It's tempting, Miss Emily. But there's my ma back in Russell County, you know. She's doing poorly, and I think she'd just plain up and die if I left her."

Emily was so touched by the man's loyalty to his mother that her eyes brimmed with tears. *You're a lucky woman, Sally Gates,* she thought, *and your bastard boy turned out to be your blessing, didn't he? I hope I'm just as fortunate.*

"Haley, I know I was only supposed to pay you six bits for the ride." Emily dug in her reticule as she spoke. "But, here. I want you to take this." She pressed a five-dollar gold piece in his hand.

"Aw, Miss Emily. That's too much."

The *Memphis Zephyr's* steam whistle gave three long, shrieking blasts, nearly deafening Emily.

"I said that's way too much," Haley shouted.

"I must run or I'll miss my boat." She bunched up her skirts and began to hasten toward the gangplank, then called back over her shoulder. "You keep that, Haley. Buy something nice for your mama."

"That's awful nice of you, Miss Emily. You have a safe trip now and you enjoy all them brand-new things out West, you hear? When you come home, I hope you'll tell me all about 'em.''

"I'll do that, Haley," she lied, trying to smile through her tears and waving from the deck while the steamboat's gangplank rose as if it, too, were waving a long and last goodbye to Mississippi and everyone in it.

Chapter Two

John Bandera was tired to the marrow of his bones. He was just back from Abilene after a hellacious late spring drive that had lost him two good men and at least two hundred head of cattle. The longhorns that had managed to survive the trip had jittered themselves to skin and bones, so instead of collecting the usual fifty bucks a head at the end of the trail, John had considered himself damned lucky to get thirty. He'd paid his men their wages, then seen to their bail when necessary, and finally settled up the considerable damages they'd wrought at four different saloons before setting out on his own, solitary, hard ride back to south Texas.

It was good to be home, he thought, as he lifted a worn and dusty boot up onto the porch rail and angled his chair onto its back legs. *Dios.* It was pure heaven to be home. Maybe he'd rename the ranch. *Pure Heaven,* maybe. Or simply *Home.*

He'd hated it six years ago when Price had insisted they name their newly acquired property The
Crippled B. John had still been hobbling around
on crutches then after breaking his leg in Arizona.
He remembered his partner's mysterious and
drunken grin when he'd slurred, "It's the perfect
name, *amigo*. Don't you see? It'll keep them
guessing which one of us it means."

"*B* for Bandera," John had muttered. "The
crippled one."

"Is it?" Price had replied. "It might just be *B*
for bastard."

Now, sitting on the porch the two of them had
built, John thought that Price probably had been
right about the ranch's name after all. It had only
taken a few months for John's busted leg to heal,
but his partner had indeed turned out to be a crippled bastard who came to despise the ranch and
the ranching along with just about everything and
everyone else in Texas, and whose only friend
turned out to be the whiskey bottle forever in his
grasp.

Then one morning, without a warning or a farewell—fond or otherwise—both the bottle and Price
McDaniel had simply disappeared. He'd sent a
wire a few months later, asking John to send him
two thousand dollars in care of a woman in Den-
ver, no doubt for one last, lethal binge. The check
had been cashed, but there hadn't been another

word from Price McDaniel. For all John knew, his partner was dead.

In the three years since Price's disappearance, John Bandera had done the work of two men— maybe even three or four—expanding The Crippled B and turning it into one of the best ranches in south Texas.

Now, though, after this grueling drive to Abilene, it was time to rest, just for a while, during the last blaze of August heat, before the autumn work began. Maybe he'd even spend a week in Brownsville or Corpus Christi, he thought. A long, slow, sleepy week in a big brass bed with rumpled sheets and a tawny *señorita* might be what he needed to ease not just his body, but his mind, as well. His heart, however, was another matter.

He sighed, squinting into the bright distance at nothing in particular, refusing to think about that, unwilling to tap into that constant, bitter ache that was forever just beneath the surface, resisting even the thought of her name. Almost. But not quite.

Emmy. *Dios,* how he loved her! How he missed her wonderful letters. He'd ridden back from Kansas hoping, almost praying, that she'd written to him one more time in spite of the fact that he'd told her not to. She hadn't written, though.

A distant swirl of dust claimed his attention. From the main house, which was built on what passed for a hill in this flat country, it was possible to see several miles in every direction. And now, near the crossing at Sweetwater Creek, John could just make out the dark silhouette of a mud wagon hitched to a pair of horses.

Damn, he thought. He'd hoped to have the house to himself for a few days, but now it looked as if his housekeeper, Señora Fuentes, and her daughter, Lupe, were coming back earlier than expected from their sojourn in Nuevo Leon.

"Damn," he muttered out loud, then hauled his weary bones out of his chair to retrieve the spyglass he kept on a table just inside the front door. The last thing he needed at the moment was a resumption of young and buxom Lupe's relentless onslaught on his senses. He never would have hired the Mexican widow last year if he'd known that the bargain included the señora's seventeen-year-old, hot-blooded daughter.

He swore again, lifting the spyglass and fitting it to his eye, prepared to see the gray head of his housekeeper and Lupe's raven waves through the open sides of the wagon. But he wasn't prepared—never in a million years—for the sudden sight of golden curls, catching the late afternoon light like sunflowers, jouncing as the mud wagon hit every bump and rut in its path.

John's heart stood absolutely still and his mouth went as dry as ash. Every nerve in his body snapped to attention as if he had just caught sight of a band of renegade Comanches riding in to pick off some of his cattle and maybe take a life or two in the process.

He swore as he ripped the telescope away, then rubbed his eye and blinked hard. Maybe he still had trail dust clogging his sight. *Madre de Dios,* let it be that. Please, let it be that. Or maybe he was so exhausted that his longtime fantasy lover had appeared before him like a blond mirage. Or maybe, more likely, he was so long lovesick that he'd finally and utterly and irretrievably lost his mind.

His hand was shaking so hard when he lifted the glass to his eye again that he was forced to raise his other hand to steady it. He scanned the landscape, sighted the wagon once again, and focused on the woman in it.

Emmy!

Damn her. Damn her to hell and back. Damn every sweet, pale yellow hair on her beautiful head. Even a mile away, he imagined he could see the bright sky-blue of her eyes, and while he was at it, he damned those, too.

Then John Bandera cursed himself and wished that he was dead. His love was coming to him, and his life was ruined.

Emily's heart was racing far faster than the matched pair of grays pulling the mud wagon. She felt as if she'd been traveling for three long years, yet it had been a mere three days since she'd boarded the steamboat in Vicksburg then transferred to a larger boat in New Orleans for her passage along the Gulf coast to Corpus Christi.

All the way her emotions had been a wild mixture of hope and fear, of bright anticipation and dark dread. But now, nearing The Crippled B Ranch, a calmness unlike any she had ever experienced seemed to settle over her. It wasn't so much that she knew how things would turn out, but that—no matter how events transpired—she was certain now that she had done the right thing in coming here.

The landscape, flat and coarse with mesquite trees and prickly pear, was exactly as Price had described it in letter after letter. Every inch of the place was surprisingly familiar, as if Emily had seen it all before. The mesquites were indeed like the sheer green lace he'd described and the sky truly did extend from east to west with hardly a cloud to mar it. Wildflowers bloomed in profusion the way he had claimed, and they did indeed combine in a huge and extraordinary carpet of reds and blues and yellows.

The grazing cattle lifted their long-horned heads when her wagon passed, gazed at her placidly, then returned to their assorted feasts. She'd seen scores of antelopes and deer, and had even glimpsed a wild boar snuffling around the twisted roots of a mesquite bush.

Everything seemed familiar because Price had taken such pains to paint wonderful, vivid pictures for her in his letters. At least he hadn't misled her in that regard. Emily felt almost as if she'd been here before. Everything was just as she'd expected.

Except the heat. It was ungodly. Hellacious. Price had written that it was hot here, but he hadn't said that a body could very nearly melt as hers had been doing all day. Of course, Price never wore petticoats nor a corset that even lightly laced felt more like hot iron bands encircling her rib cage.

The man who was slouching up front driving the ramshackle mud wagon wore a wide-brimmed hat to shade himself, but even so his plaid shirt was soaked through with perspiration. Emily didn't feel all that much sympathy for him, however, since he'd charged her an outrageous sum to take her the thirty-five miles from Corpus Christi to The Crippled B. He hadn't said more than three or four gruff words to her since departing the coastal town, and Emily had found herself longing for the cozy chatter of Haley Gates and wondering a little sadly what he was doing right now back in Mississippi. Home seemed so far behind her. And ahead? She hadn't the faintest idea.

For a moment then, for a frightened heartbeat, her courage failed her. This southern part of Texas, this land of new beginnings was dangerous, a harsh place with thorns on its lacy trees and four-foot-wide horns on its cows. Mississippi seemed civilized, even gentle, in comparison. Safe, too. Perhaps she should have stayed home in spite of the coming scandal. At least people there knew her and cared about her, if only enough to gossip.

This driver was the first real Texan she had met, and not only was he sullen, but he didn't seem too familiar with the territory, either. When she pointed out landmarks that Price had mentioned—the Culley ranch with its twisted fences or a particularly lovely grove of live oaks—the driver would just shrug and mumble that they'd soon be getting there.

And now they were. They were here. Emily's heart fairly clanged in her chest when the horses' hooves rattled the boards that spanned Sweetwater Creek. Unlike the green and rippling creeks back home, this one was just a narrow river of dust right now as it waited for the winter rains. Her mouth went as dry as the creek.

Then, suddenly, catching sight of Price's house atop a rise in the distance, Emily forgot to be afraid. The sun was setting behind the two-story frame structure with the covered front porch, setting it off like a little jewel against a background of brilliant reds and pinks and oranges. It was exactly as she had pictured it. No. It was better...

…because, standing on the front porch, she could see a man with a spyglass trained in her direction. Was it Price? *Oh, please,* she prayed. *Let it be Price. Let him call me Emmy. Don't let him turn me away. Don't let him turn* us *away.*

Señora Fuentes's chickens squawked and scattered when the mud wagon clattered into the yard. In the corral, the horses came to the near rail to sniff the changing currents in the air and to investigate the newcomers. But none was so curious as John Bandera as he stood leaning against a porch rail, arms crossed over his chest and his right leg cocked in a casual pose that belied the turmoil in his gut and the panic in his brain.

He had decided to lie. If he knew anything, he knew that much. He would tell the woman—his beloved Emmy—that Price was still away in Abilene, that his return was uncertain. Beyond that, he hadn't the slightest notion what he'd say or do.

But the lie was a good enough place to start. It was the only place. Later, when he was able to think more clearly, he would figure out how to construct a tangled web around it. Right now all he could do was stare stupefied at the woman in the back of the wagon.

She was here! She was real! He couldn't quite believe it.

She was his treasured *carte de visite* come to

lovely life. Her hair was more golden, more glorious than he'd ever thought to imagine. Her eyes were round and deep and beautiful as cornflowers. Her skin was as pale and luminous as dawn.

Six or seven years had passed since the image he treasured had been captured, and those years had added a sensuous fullness to her mouth that hadn't been there before, as well as a healthy, feminine roundness to the rest of her. Emily Russell was more beautiful than John had ever dared dream, and for a minute he found himself wishing she had turned out ugly or deformed in a way that had been disguised in her photograph. He damned her again for being beautiful.

"Hey, you," the driver called from his seat on the wagon. "This woman is looking for The Crippled B Ranch."

"She's found it," John said, slowly straightening up and heading down the porch steps, his gaze fixed on Emily the way a compass fixes on north while he tried to maintain a neutral expression. It wasn't easy, pretending he didn't recognize the love of his life, ignoring the heartbeats that were about to hammer a hole right through the front of his shirt.

"Then you're McDaniel?" the driver asked.

"No. I'm..."

"John Bandera," Emily called happily, leaning

out the mud wagon's open window. "I'd know you anywhere, I believe, from Price's description."

When she extended a white gloved hand toward him, John felt his own hand drawn to hers like filings to a magnet.

"I'm Emily Russell," she said. "From Russell County, Mississippi. Perhaps Price has mentioned me?"

John nodded. Then, suddenly aware that he had held her hand too long for a mere hello, he let go and stepped back.

"I know he isn't expecting me." She was looking around the ranch now, her blue eyes sparkling with delight.

"Price isn't here."

He might as well have said that Price was dead for the way the delight dulled in her eyes and the happiness drained from her expression.

She sat back. "Wh-where…?"

"In Abilene."

"Abilene?" The way she said it the Kansas cow town sounded distant as a planet. "And when…?"

"I don't expect him back for quite some time, Miss Russell."

"I see."

No, she didn't see at all, Emily thought. Disappointment was fairly crushing her, squeezing her heart and turning her brain into a tight, aching knot. "I've come so far. Such a long way." Her own voice sounded even farther away.

"You staying or going, lady?" the driver asked impatiently. "If you're going back to Corpus, it'll cost you triple, seeing as how it's gonna be dark pretty soon."

Emily didn't answer. Staying? Going? She barely understood the meaning of the words, much less how they pertained to her. Dark? Was it? She felt numb all of a sudden, and dumb. For a moment she wondered if a sunstroke had robbed her of her ability to speak and to move.

The driver was angled around in his seat, staring at her, his eyes mere slits beneath his twisted brows. John Bandera was staring at her, too, but there was no reading his dark face. He might as well have been a cigar store Indian with rigid, wooden lips and deep, expressionless eyes.

"Well?" the driver snapped. "What's it going to be, lady? You staying or going? I ain't got all day." He tapped a restless boot on the floorboards.

"She's staying."

Now, with a scowl carved deeply into his face, John Bandera reached for her valise, then the carpetbags and the big steamer trunk, and finally—not quite so roughly—for Emily herself.

"Come on," he said, his big hands circling her waist, lifting her up and out and setting her down before she was even aware that she was moving.

"How much does she owe you?" he asked the driver.

"Already paid for the one-way trip," the man replied.

"Fine." Having said that, Bandera slapped the haunch of the horse closest to him. "So long, then," he said, stepping back and drawing Emily with him as the wagon took off with such a lurch that the driver nearly pitched backward over his wooden seat.

They stood there a moment, the two of them, in the tan cloud of dust the horses had kicked up, watching the mud wagon bumping wildly away while the driver tried to hold on to his hat and the reins.

Go? Stay? Emily really hadn't made up her mind yet, but here she was anyway. She wondered if the driver would hear her if she called him back.

But just then, without a word, Price's scowling partner picked up her valise and wedged it under one arm before he collected her heavy trunk and both carpetbags. Still silent, he turned and headed toward the house with all of her worldly possessions.

Emily, obviously unwelcome, followed slowly in John Bandera's wake.

"You'll be comfortable in here. For now, anyway." John dropped the carpetbags on Señora Fuentes's quilt-covered bed. "My housekeeper and her daughter are off in Mexico for a while," he said, then quickly corrected himself. "Our housekeeper, I mean."

"That would be Mrs. Fuentes," she said, standing in the doorway. "Price has written me about her. About her chickens and her garden and her daughter, Lupe." She laughed softly. "Why, I almost feel as if I've met them both."

Still with his back to her, John closed his eyes and drew in a deep breath. *Dios*. This wasn't going to work. His brain was already dizzy from trying to keep things straight and his tongue was tangling around every word he spoke.

He should have sent her away. He should have paid the damned driver his triple fare and had him take the woman back to Corpus Christi. He should have said, "Price McDaniel's gone, lady. Long gone. Chances are good he's dead. Your trip was for naught. *Adios*." That, after all, was the truth.

"It was kind of you to let me stay, Mr. Bandera."

She was right behind him now, so close that if he turned he could take her in his arms the way he'd longed to do, ached to do, year after year, night after night after night.

When he did turn, she stepped back, obviously uncomfortable, perhaps even afraid. He was a stranger, after all. He wasn't Price.

"You're probably hungry, Miss Russell," he said. "I'll fix us something to eat."

"That would be wonderful." She was pulling off her gloves now, one dainty finger at a time. "I wish you'd call me Emily. I feel as if I've known you long enough and well enough, Mr. Bandera, to call you by your Christian name. May I? John?"

"Sure," he said. "Why not?"

She tossed her gloves on the bed. "Good." Then she started plucking the pins from her prim little hat. "You'll think this strange perhaps, John," she said, "but this place, The Crippled B, feels more like my home in many ways than Mississippi ever did."

John didn't respond. He was already on his way out of the room, hurrying, fleeing, before his Emmy pulled the last pin loose and uncovered all those glorious golden curls.

Exhausted as she was, Emily lay awake for a long time that night in the housekeeper's narrow bed with its starched muslin sheets and ancient, threadbare quilt. She tried with all her might to think about Price, but her mind kept returning to John Bandera. What a peculiar man he was, and not in the least as Price had described him.

She recalled one particular letter in which Price had referred to his partner as a mongrel. Emily had written back, asking for details. "His mother was

a Comanche,'' Price had replied. ''As for his father, I assume the man was white, light-eyed, and
quite tall—as John is over six feet—and the culprit
was probably fleet of foot since he didn't stick
around to even witness the birth of his child.''

''Bandera's a man of few words,'' another letter
had said. Having met John now, Emily thought that
was an exaggeration. He was a man of fewer than
few words. It was her impression this evening that
speech was almost painful for him and that he was
grateful for their frequent lapses into silence, and
then thoroughly relieved when it came time to say
good-night.

A very peculiar man. And at the same time an
extraordinarily handsome man whose features
seemed to blend the very best of his diverse blood-
lines. His long, dark Indian hair had the merest
suggestion of curl, a gift of his father no doubt,
along with the amber light that glowed in his dark
eyes. His features weren't finely sculpted the way
Price's were, but rather ruggedly chiseled from
brow to jaw.

He was as different from Price as night from
day, and yet there had been a time or two during
their meal when John had somehow reminded her
of Price, not in looks but in his speech. Not that
there was so much of that, but once or twice he'd
used a word or turned a phrase that sounded un-
cannily like Price. It probably shouldn't have sur-

prised her, though, since the two of them had been together—in the Army and now at The Crippled B—for eight years or so. It only made sense that they would pick up each other's habits, mannerisms, and patterns of speech.

She fell asleep finally, wondering what Price's voice sounded like and if it was as deep as John Bandera's and if the Mississippian she loved so well had acquired the subtle Spanish accent that made the sound of his partner's voice so sensuous and exotic.

He may have been a man of few words, but those few were certainly like music.

Chapter Three

The Crippled B's beautiful, but uninvited guest slept late the following morning, for which John was grateful since it gave him some additional and very necessary time to get not only his house in order, but his mind as well.

The night before, after Emily had gone to bed, John had gathered up all of her letters, along with her photograph in its hammered tin frame, then locked them away in the safe where he kept the deeds to all his property and the cash he kept on hand to meet the monthly payroll.

Right now there wasn't anybody to pay, thank God, or to tell Emily Russell that they hadn't seen hide nor hair of Price McDaniel in three years. John decided that he didn't have much cause to worry about Señora Fuentes or her daughter, Lupe, since neither one of them spoke more than one or two words of English.

As far as he knew, Emily's knowledge of Spanish was limited to a few assorted words he'd written in a couple of his letters to her. Besides, Price had left long before John had hired the housekeeper. As far as he knew, Señora Fuentes and her daughter didn't even know his missing partner's name.

It was different, though, with some of the longtime ranch hands, the ones who'd been around from the beginning of The Crippled B. Fortunately, two of the old-timers, Diego and Hector, only knew enough English to order a halfway decent meal in an Abilene cafe. But then there was Tater Latham. The lanky Kansan not only spoke English, but spoke it at such length and at such great volume that people were always telling him to shut up. Tater, when he returned, could be a problem.

The obvious solution, of course, was sending Emily back to her home in Mississippi. And during a long night with hardly any sleep, John had decided to do just that. Send the beautiful Miss Russell back to Russell County where she belonged.

But not yet.

Dios, not just yet.

Although he had fallen in love with his Emmy's words on paper, it had only taken him moments to realize that those words had been a perfect reflection of the flesh-and-blood woman. She was as bright as she was beautiful. As kind as she was fair.

She was a lady through and through, and yet far more sensuous than he'd ever have believed with her full lips and her direct blue gaze. Her accent reminded him of Price, but his partner's voice had been salted with sarcasm while Emily's flowed like the sweetest clover honey.

And lady that she was, she'd given him not the slightest indication that the color of his skin offended her or his accent grated on her ears or his lack of proper parentage affected her at all. She seemed oblivious to any difference.

Last evening John had even caught himself studying her calm expression and thinking that maybe it didn't matter to his Emmy one bit that he wasn't a blue-eyed, fair-haired, fine-blooded gentleman like Price. But, of course, it had to matter. How could it not? Miss Emily Russell of Russell County, Mississippi, was just too kind and too polite, too much of a lady, to allow her disdain and her distaste to show.

"You're a damned fool," John muttered to himself. *"Loco. Estupido."*

He swore again as he jerked open the center drawer of the desk, withdrawing a sheet of paper to make a list of supplies they'd be needing soon for The Crippled B. Maybe, he hoped, tallying pounds of flour and salt and chicken feed, and figuring yards of hemp rope and muslin and wire would take his mind off the woman who was sleeping nearby in Señora Fuentes's bed.

He'd only managed to write a few items on the page when he heard her honey voice.

"Good morning, John."

She seemed to float into the front room, her blue silk wrapper whisking about her legs and her golden hair spilling over her shoulders like warm morning sunshine. Then she stood still, staring at the desktop.

"Oh, you're busy writing. I'm so sorry, John. I didn't intend to interrupt you."

"No. It's all right. You're not interrupting at all. I was just…"

The words stuck in his throat all of a sudden when he looked down at the list and the dark, distinctive penmanship there. Had she seen it? With a flick of his wrist, he turned the telltale paper over.

"This can wait," he told her, putting down the pen and rising from his chair.

Emily continued to stare at the desk, though, with a wistful slant to her mouth and an odd, distracted light in her eyes.

"I was just thinking about Price," she said almost dreamily. "I imagine this is where he sits when he composes letters, isn't it?" She gestured to the chair John had just left.

He shrugged. "Maybe. I don't know."

She moved forward then, reached for the steel pen he'd only just put down, and held it delicately, as if it might break from a mere touch.

"You must think me very silly to be so sentimental about an inanimate object like this. It's just…" She clutched the pen tighter. Her eyes shone with tears. "When do you think Price will be returning from Kansas? Will it be days? Weeks?"

"I don't know." *Never,* he longed to say. *Jamas.*

Under the golden shawl of her hair, John could see her delicate shoulders slump a fraction. He ached to take her in his arms, to comfort her. He had to clench his fists to keep his hands from reaching out. She was so fragile just then, so pale and vulnerable, and he thought of how Price had described the Southern belles he claimed to know so well. *Gardenias,* he'd called them. *Touch them and they bruise.*

Emily put the pen down with exquisite care, sighed, and then turned to him, attempting to smile.

"Well, enough of that. Nobody likes a sad and weepy female for a guest, do they? I'll try to be better company, John. I promise. Now, don't let me take up any more of your time. I don't want to keep you from your work."

He shrugged again. "There's not so much of that this time of year."

He wished there were. He wished he had a ton of work to distract him. A score of horses to be broken. A hundred mavericks to be branded. A thousand back-breaking chores. Anything to put some distance between himself and this woman. Maybe that wasn't such a bad idea. Distance.

"I was planning to ride out today and check on a few of the line shacks," he said. "To see if they need repairs."

Emily was gazing at him so intently now, such bright curiosity shining in her eyes, that he found himself uttering words he'd never intended.

"You could come along if you want. With me, I mean. See some of the ranch."

Then, before he could take the invitation back, Emily's whole face fairly glowed. "Oh, I'd love that," she said. "I'll hurry and get dressed."

Emily surveyed as much of herself as possible in the little mirror that hung between Señora Fuentes's wooden crucifix and a candle sconce. She'd laced her corset as loosely as she could before putting on her lightest gabardine dress. She looked healthy and plump, she decided, rather than three, nearly four months pregnant. And she was looking forward to her excursion around The Crippled B.

"Best bring some extra belongings," John had told her, and when she'd raised an eyebrow, he had added, "This is Texas. We may not make it back tonight."

She had simply nodded in agreement, and now she wondered why the prospect of overnighting in the wilds with a near stranger—half Indian, at that—didn't bother her in the least. Quite the contrary as a matter of fact. She was looking forward to seeing as much as possible of Price's ranch and, somewhere deep inside her, in some curious little corner, she was looking forward to being with John Bandera, listening to his deep, Spanish-accented voice, stingy though he was with it, and looking into his dark amber eyes.

"Why, Emily Russell, you shameless hussy!"

She grinned at her own reflection in the mirror, thinking that being out West had already stripped her of more than a few constraints of polite society. There was the loose corset, of course, but that was a necessity in her condition. But she had also brushed out her hair and pulled it back with a blue ribbon, something she never would have done back home. Nor would she have found herself so drawn to a man who was little more than a stranger. Or attracted to anyone, for that matter.

The incident with Alvin Gibbons had had nothing to do with physical attraction, but everything to do with her broken heart and devastated hopes. There hadn't been a second she'd spent with Alvin that she hadn't wished that he were Price. On the night that they made love, she almost managed to convince herself that he truly *was* Price.

Funny, she thought. All of a sudden she didn't feel so brokenhearted anymore or quite so hopeless. No doubt that was because she was here, at The Crippled B, surrounded by Price's land and his possessions. Now, if only Price himself were here, everything would be perfect. Or almost.

She smiled softly, remembering the feel of his pen in her hand a while earlier. That little piece of steel and all the poetry that had flowed from it had changed her life, she thought. She could only pray now that it was for better rather than worse.

Then she sighed, picked up the carpetbag she'd packed, and went to meet John Bandera for their excursion.

John had already stacked an assortment of lumber and tools in the wagon bed. Then, just as he was lifting a keg of nails, he caught sight of Emily coming from the back of the house. He nearly dropped twenty pounds of iron right on his toes.

She looked so pretty and prim in her tan getup with all its pleats and swags and bows. Like a little birthday cake swirled with pale chocolate icing. Like the best of birthday gifts. He had to firm his lips against the smile that was itching across them.

"You can't wear that hat," he said almost gruffly as she approached, narrowing his eyes on the straw and velvet concoction atop her head. "You'll burn to a crisp. This is—"

"Texas! Yes, I know." She laughed as she brought a beige silk parasol from behind her skirt, then snapped it open and lifted it above her head. "There. Will that do, John?"

He grinned in spite of himself, thinking he'd never seen anything quite so charming or half as silly. "Fine with me, if you want to hold that umbrella for ten or twelve hours."

"It might even shade us both," she said.

John had no intention of sitting that close. Where the hell had his head been when he'd conjured up this trip, then suggested she come along? Hell, if he'd used his head six years earlier instead of his heart, if he'd never sent that first fateful letter, he wouldn't be in this situation now, would he?

While Emily waited in the dainty shade of her parasol, he finished loading the wagon. He tossed his saddle in and then brought his favorite mare from the corral, slipped the bridle over her head, and secured the reins to the tailgate.

"That's it," he said. "Let's go."

She stood on the opposite side of the wagon, smiling pleasantly, twirling her parasol, making no effort to move. He found himself staring at her stupidly while it slowly dawned on him that it had been a while since he'd been with a person hindered by her own clothes, one who required assistance getting into, out of, up on, down from, and around.

Madre de Dios. That meant he was going to have to assist her, to act as if he wasn't terrified to clasp his hands about her waist, to feel the size and the warmth of her through her dress when he lifted her up. And then he was going to have to let her go, to pretend that touching her meant nothing to him at all when it meant everything, when it was all that he'd longed to do and dreamed about for years.

For a second John was tempted to unload the wagon and drag all the lumber and tools back into the barn, to tell Emily the weather looked bad or the horse looked lame or the axle looked cracked or any excuse he could conjure up to stay here, not to have to put his hands on her.

Caught in his quandary, John didn't immediately notice that Emily had already taken matters—as well as her skirt—into her own hands. She had collapsed the little umbrella in order to grasp the back of the wagon seat to haul herself up, but in another second it was going to be confounded Emily who collapsed if he didn't help.

John sprinted around the rear of the wagon and got his hands up just as she was coming down, then he stood there—half dazed and wholly mute—with his arms full of his Emmy, her twenty yards of skirts and petticoats, and her damn blasted parasol.

The little shriek she'd uttered when first falling turned into a bright peal of laughter now and her blue eyes sparkled up into his, reminding him of high mountain lakes and wide summer skies and how much he'd loved the sense of humor that always came through in her letters, making him laugh out loud when he read them. He wanted to laugh now in concert with Emily, but he didn't. He didn't dare.

Instead, he let out a scorching curse in Spanish before he growled, "You need to be more careful. You almost broke your blasted neck."

She blinked at his harsh tone and her laughter stopped immediately. The light in her eyes darkened. The lovely sparkle disappeared.

He shifted her abruptly in his arms, then lofted her brusquely onto the seat. "Hang on, will you? It's a long drop to the ground."

Emily nodded, thinking suddenly that the drop was longer and more treacherous than John could know for someone in her delicate condition, a fact that she'd breezily ignored when she'd attempted to climb into the wagon without his aid.

Ever since her arrival in Texas, she'd felt young and adventurous. That wasn't good. At twenty-six, she wasn't all that young. At more than three months gone with child, she shouldn't feel the least inclined to adventure. In any condition, she shouldn't be so excited about the prospect of an excursion with a man she barely knew.

What would people in Russell County think of her outrageous behavior? What would Price think when he learned that she had gone off so cavalierly with his partner? Surely he wouldn't approve.

But no sooner had that idea struck her, than she realized just how ludicrous it was to worry about Price's or anybody's approval or disapproval. Her reputation was already ruined. She was already a fallen woman. All things considered, how much farther was there for her to tumble?

Emily snapped open her parasol and positioned it over her head just as the wagon seat canted leftward, pressing her—shoulder to thigh—against John for a moment before he shifted away.

"You ready?" he asked.

For what? Emily thought suddenly before she nodded an enthusiastic yes.

"*Vamanos,*" John said, and his big, dark hands gently flicked the reins.

By three that afternoon the sun was still beating down on them like a white-hot hammer. To the west, mirages pooled in the distance under miles of dry mesquite. To the south, however, the sky had been darkening ominously for the past hour and now it was taking on a sickly greenish cast that John didn't like one bit.

Emily wasn't faring too well in this heat, in his opinion, even though she kept protesting that she was used to it back home in Mississippi. They'd stopped for a bit to eat at noon, but after a single hard-boiled egg she'd begun to look queasy. When she excused herself and disappeared around a live oak, John was fairly sure he heard that hard-boiled egg coming right back up.

Now, with what looked to be a good-sized storm moving toward them, he cursed himself once more for bringing her along. He should have kept a weather eye on the sky instead of a lover's eye on her. He should have considered her comfort instead of his own misguided desire to be close to her. She wasn't some sturdy, rawboned farm girl, used to scorching heat and hardships. She was, as Price had said, a gardenia. And even though John had never seen one of those, he could well imagine their pale delicacy after seeing Emily.

He wrenched his gaze from the approaching storm to look at her now, and her eyes met his as frankly as they always did, while her mouth curved into a lovely and contented smile.

"I'm so enjoying this, John. It's hard to believe we've been traveling for over five hours and we're still on your land." Her smile grew even lovelier and warmer. "You and Price have done very well for yourselves."

"I guess," he said. "It's not so hard, though, when one partner's all money and the other's all muscle."

She gave him an odd look then, and John immediately realized he was quoting directly from a letter he had written her several years ago. A letter *Price* had written her.

"That's what Price always said, anyway," he added quickly. "What he says, I mean."

Damnation! He was digging himself in deeper every time he opened his mouth. There was so much he couldn't say that he couldn't even begin to remember it all.

"Price loves this place," she said. "Maybe he didn't at first, but I've gotten the impression over the years that The Crippled B truly has come to be his home. I suspect it's the same for you."

"Do you?"

She nodded. "I've been watching you today. Watching the way your eyes fairly drink in the landscape. The way you smile at the young calves chasing after their mothers and at the deer when they disappear into the brush. I saw the worry in your eyes when you pointed out those coyote tracks a few miles back."

Now she tilted a little grin at him and wagged a finger. "You can't fool me, John Bandera."

"No?"

"No. You love this place every bit as much as Price does."

"Maybe," he said, remembering how his missing partner came to hate the dust that settled over everything and the relentless heat and, toward the end, even the sight of a longhorn. Price had even started talking about going back to Mississippi— the lesser of two evils, he had claimed—before he suddenly took off for parts unknown and no doubt just as evil once he arrived.

Emily closed her parasol now, for the sun had been obliterated by thick, churning clouds. A gust of wind tugged at her hair ribbon. "One thing Price mentioned that he especially loves here is being able to see weather coming in. He says… Oh, how did he describe it? That it's a little like watching a herd of buffalo stampeding across the sky." Her gaze lifted. "He's right. I can see it for myself. It does look like a great wild herd of buffalo."

Green buffalo, John thought. Fierce ones, too, and coming on fast. He and Emily were about to be trampled by their thundering hooves. He thought briefly of whipping the horse and trying to outrun the storm, but he realized it was no use. Though he'd only been in one twister before, years ago in Indian Territory, he'd learned only too well that you didn't run from these wind devils. You hid.

The roiling clouds were beginning to dip all around them now and the wind was starting to pick up dust and dead leaves and dry sticks. The pressure in his ears shifted suddenly, and just then a bolt of lightning split the sky to the south, then another, and another.

He pulled the wagon up, and at the same time did a quick and desperate reckoning of the terrain. The dry, narrow bed of an arroyo lay just a hundred feet or so to the left. They could make it—maybe—if they ran.

Chapter Four

"Maybe we should crawl under the wagon," Emily called out to him over the fury of the rising wind.

"Too dangerous," John called back.

He was quickly undoing the reins he'd tethered to the tailgate in order to free his wild-eyed, panicky saddle horse. There wasn't going to be time to unhitch the luckless gelding up front. Then, when the first hailstones pounded down on his shoulders and the brim of his hat, he realized there was barely time to make it to the creek bed.

Emily was a tangle of windblown skirts trying frantically and unsuccessfully to climb down from the wagon seat, when he reached her.

"Here. Come on."

With one swift and not-so-gentle motion, John wrenched her down onto the ground, then propelled her in the direction of the creek.

The whole world had gone a wet and queasy green around them with long, skittish bolts of blue lightning striking ever closer and the resultant thunderclaps almost deafening them now. Hailstones, big as babies' fists, bounced around them as they ran, and turned the ground beneath them treacherously slick.

Emily's face was pale and her eyes were huge with terror as she stumbled along beside him. *Dios!* She had every right to be terrified. He suspected his own dark face went a few shades paler when he glimpsed the caroming, twisting, screaming cloud that was riding down on them.

Once they reached the arroyo, John didn't stand on ceremony. He pushed Emily facedown in the shallow ditch, then immediately threw himself on top of her, trying his best to hunch his shoulders and arms over her head, to create whatever barrier he could between the woman and the storm. He twisted his fingers in some exposed roots and held on for all he was worth.

The tornado sounded like a locomotive at full throttle when it blasted by. John couldn't tell exactly how close it was, but its winds pulled at his shirttail and pant legs as if they meant to strip him naked or even to the bone.

All the while, the hard, frozen rain was battering him relentlessly. Some of the hailstones felt more like boulders or cannonballs when they slammed into him, so he tried to flatten himself even more to keep Emily out of the line of fire.

"It's all right, Emily," he whispered close to her ear. "I won't let anything hurt you."

His words were as much to reassure himself as they were to comfort her, for John wasn't sure how long he could keep from being ripped away by the fierce winds or withstand the heavy onslaught of the hail or even keep his own weight from crushing the delicate body pressed into the ditch beneath him.

It had probably been two dozen years since he'd been inside a church, more than that since he last confessed his sins to a *padre,* but now the words of the *Ave Maria* came back to him and he whispered them again and again, adding a prayer of his own.

Santa Maria, por favor, do not let us perish here. Or take me, if you must take someone, but let this woman live.

The storm roared over them like a fast freight train, and then, just as quickly as it had emerged, it disappeared. The hard hail reverted to a soft rain and the brutal winds dwindled to a wet breeze. The lightning and the thunder ceased. A few feeble rays of sunshine fingered through the clouds.

"Thank God," Emily breathed into the wet sleeve that was still shielding her head. Only now was she truly aware of the warm weight upon her. She tried in vain to move, to turn.

"John?" It came as no surprise that her voice was trembling along with all the rest of her. "John, are you all right?"

He shifted a bit, but it was another moment before he answered. "Fine. You? Are you all right?"

"Yes, I think so. My God, that was close."

He grunted in reply—"Too close!"—and rolled to his left, allowing Emily to sit up. After she blinked the grit from her eyes and looked around, all she could do was moan softly. "Oh, my God."

For as far as she could see in every direction, the ground was covered with white balls of ice, some of them almost as big around as grapefruits. She'd seen hail before but never anything bigger than peas or marbles. This was the eeriest sight she'd ever witnessed as the sun began to filter through the clouds and to glisten on the bleak ice field around them.

Why, the landscape was so pearly white they could have been on the moon, for all she knew. Where in the world was the wagon? And where were the horses? Where was...well...everything? Even the few mesquite trees still standing nearby were bent in the direction of the storm and nearly barren of their leaves.

Emily tried to stand up only to discover that her

liquid knees would not support her, so she collapsed back in a heap of wet and muddy skirts.

"Here." John had gotten to his feet and now he extended his open hand to her. "Come on."

His grip was warm and firm when he pulled her up, but as he did, Emily heard his sharp intake of breath and the Spanish curse he bit off.

"What is it, John?"

"It's nothing. I'm okay." His amber eyes searched her face, before his gaze traveled the length of her. "And you? No broken bones? Bruises?"

Emily shook her head and tried to mount a small smile. "Just quaking knees. That was the worst storm I've ever seen. It's a miracle we weren't killed."

He was surveying the landscape around them now, glaring at the chunks of ice as if they were animate things still capable of doing damage. His breathing, Emily noticed, was shallow and his lips drawn together in a hard line. She could tell he was in pain, and could see that he was trying to conceal it from her.

"John?"

He swore softly again and stepped up out of the little, ice-covered creek bed. "Come on. If you're steady enough to walk, we'll look for the horses and the wagon. It won't be long before it gets too dark to find them."

"I'm steady enough," she said. "But you—"

"Good," he said, cutting her off. He grasped her elbow then to keep her from slipping on the melting carpet of ice. "Let's go."

The sun was just about to slide over the western horizon and darkness was coming on fast from the east when John finally, grudgingly admitted defeat.

They weren't going to find the wagon, and even if they did manage to locate it, it wasn't going to be in one piece. The damn thing had probably been blown to bits, and all of those bits were probably whirled and scattered over five counties. He didn't even want to consider the whereabouts of his favorite mare or the fate of the poor gelding.

Nor did he want to think too much about his own condition. As the hours progressed and his pain increased substantially, he'd concluded that one of those cannonball hailstones had broken at least one of his ribs. It was his punishment, no doubt, for bringing Emily along today and putting her in harm's way. And now he'd be paying even more for his crime tonight when they'd have to sleep here, in the open, together.

He'd have paid double the contents of his safe right now for a bottle of tequila to ease his pain and to turn his thoughts away from the woman who'd been walking by his side for the last few hours, uncomplaining, even cheerful, in contrast to his increasingly black mood.

"We'll stop here," he told her.

"Yes," she answered with a sigh. "I suppose we should."

She sounded tired now, more than John had realized. Even so, she managed to smile.

"I've never camped out before, you know." She looked up at the darkening sky. "I've never slept under the stars."

He knew. It was something they'd discussed back and forth in their letters. She envied him, she'd written, for being able to sleep under heaven's starry canopy. And John had often dreamed about just this, sharing these same stars with his Emmy and introducing her to Polaris and Cassiopeia and Orion, one arm draped around her delicate shoulders and the other arm pointing skyward, knowing it would never happen. Only now it was.

"It's not all it's cracked up to be," he said gruffly. "I'll have you back to the house tomorrow. Back to a decent bed." And then, just under his breath, he added, "I'm sorry."

"Sorry!" she exclaimed. "Why, John Bandera, I honestly believe you're holding yourself personally responsible for the storm. It's little wonder you and Price make such good partners. I believe he'd have a similar reaction."

She wagged a finger at him, then laughed gaily. "But Price has assured me that sleeping out under the stars is better than any church for being close to God."

Recognizing his own heartfelt words, John scowled. "I didn't know my partner was such a philosopher."

"I'm sure there's quite a lot about him you don't know." There was no smugness in her voice. Merely certainty. And an undisguised affection. "I believe men tend to open up their feelings more readily to the opposite sex."

"Maybe so."

She gave him a look that was part pity, part female curiosity. "I take it, then, that you've never *philosophized* or shared any of your tender feelings with another?"

"You take it any way you see fit, Emily. Me and my tender feelings need to gather up some firewood now before it's too dark."

He stalked away from her as well as a man with a bashed rib cage could stalk. By the time he'd gathered ample brush and had coaxed it into a decent fire, John could feel the flames warming the sheen of sweat on his face. His side felt as if there was an arrow buried deep within it. There was no use ignoring it anymore, or pretending that he wasn't hurt and even in some degree of danger. If that invisible arrow of a rib were to shift and puncture his lung, his Emmy was going to be in big trouble.

He lowered himself gingerly to the ground and began to unbutton his shirt just as Emily came up behind him with an armload of brush.

"I knew it," she exclaimed, dropping her bundle of firewood and then dropping herself in a heap of skirts beside him. "You *are* injured, John. What is it? How bad is it? What can I do to help?"

She laid a gentle hand on his shoulder and the touch instantly reverberated throughout John's body. Now, in addition to his broken rib and bruised muscles, he suffered the piercing and indescribable pain of desire.

"It's not so serious," he said, trying not to wince when he eased his shirttails from under his belt. "Just a bruised rib, I think. I'm going to tear up my shirt and use it as a binding."

"You'll do no such thing." She shot to her feet. "I won't allow it."

He gritted his teeth, then lofted his gaze to the starry sky, seeking the patience he didn't feel just then. He was aching too damn much to spare Miss Emily Russell's delicate feelings of politeness and prudery.

"Look," he said bluntly, "I'm a stranger to you. I know that. And I know it isn't polite or fitting to take off my shirt in front of you. But you're going to have to trust me about this, Emily. It's very, very necessary.''

''That wasn't what I meant, John.''

She was standing behind him so he couldn't see her expression or just what she was doing, but the next sounds he heard were the unmistakable rustlings of a woman divesting herself of a petticoat or two.

''What I meant was,'' she continued, ''that it's foolish for you to rip up your shirt when I have all this silk and muslin doing nothing but puffing out my skirt.''

She plopped back down beside him, her arms full of white lacy garments. ''There. You see? Now, please just tell me how wide I should tear the strips.''

Her voice, as well as the brass tack glitter in her eyes, brooked no argument, so John held up his thumb and forefinger, indicating a decent width for a bandage.

''Two inches, give or take, I'd say,'' he murmured.

''All right.'' She began ripping. And ripping. No sooner had she shredded one petticoat than she began on the other. John watched in appreciative silence while her fingers fairly flew. In a matter of minutes, she was done with the ripping and had begun knotting the lacy strips together.

He stole a glance or two at her determined face.

Her mouth was a study in purposefulness, and when her tongue peeked out a fraction to wet her lips, he felt his body tighten instantly at the sight. The thought of how he'd react if he actually kissed those lips made his mouth so dry he almost couldn't speak. Not the words he wanted to say, anyway.

"I'm grateful, Emily," he said at last. "I'll repay you for your loss as soon as we get back to the ranch."

"Nonsense. I'll be glad not to have to carry the weight of these petticoats on our walk tomorrow." She pulled the final white knot tight. "There. Now let's get you out of that shirt."

He started to shrug out of it on his own, but then there were her hands all of a sudden and her cool fingertips guiding him, gliding down his back and arms while her mouth made all sorts of soft and sympathetic little noises.

"Oh, you poor dear," she exclaimed. "I've never seen such bruises. Especially here."

Her light touch on the site of his injured rib was as exquisite as it was painful. John sucked in his breath.

"I can manage," he said, reaching for one end of the long knotted strip.

Emily jerked it out of his hand. "I'm sure you can, but I suspect I'll manage better. Just tell me whether it's too tight. It should be tight, shouldn't it, if it's to do you any good?''

She was already beginning to wind the petticoat strips around his chest, her hair brushing his skin, her breath warm and sweet on his cheek, his neck, his shoulders. For a moment John felt almost guilty, as if he had deliberately conjured up the violent storm and its aftermath for the sole sake of this moment of intimacy. He closed his eyes the better to savor it. He'd dreamed of this—her!—so very long.

"There." She wove the ragged end of the bandage through the strips already in place. "That ought to do it. For now at least."

John drew in a tentative breath, deeper than the shallow ones he'd been practicing for the last few hours. It was better. He let the breath out as a rough sigh of relief.

"Much better," he said. "*Muchas gracias,* Emily. I'm in your debt."

She sat back now and laughed. "*De nada,* John. Did I say that right?''

He nodded, trying to suppress a smile.

"Anyway," she continued, "I don't think Price would ever forgive me if I didn't do all I could for his partner when he was in trouble, do you?''

He could feel his expression alter and hoped she wouldn't be able to read the disappointment that seemed to wash over his face at the mention of

Price's name. Their moment of intimacy, so precious to John, had just blown away like smoke.

"I think Price would forgive you of anything," he said softly, avoiding her eyes and the firelight dancing in them, thinking he himself could forgive her anything, everything, most of all her anger and bitterness toward him when she learned the truth.

Emily feigned sleep, and at the same time pretended to be oblivious of her human pillow.

An hour ago John had insisted that she get some sleep. "If you don't," he'd told her rather sternly, "you won't be able to put one foot in front of the other tomorrow, and I won't be able to carry you. Just lie down and close your eyes for a little while. Here." He'd patted his leg. "Consider me just a pillow."

Some pillow, she thought, with its rough woolen cover and its stuffing of muscle and bone. The mattress beneath her was tough grass still a little wet from the storm and earth as hard as iron.

There were stars, though, by the thousands. But this wasn't quite what Emily had imagined all those nights when she dreamed about sleeping out under the stars. Those starry fantasies had included a tent, a cot, and a modicum of bedding. They had included Price, as well, but here she was on the hard ground with her head pillowed on John Bandera's equally hard, muscular thigh.

With his legs crossed Indian style, he sat so still he might have been mistaken for a tree stump. Well…a handsome tree stump. She'd been peeking through her lashes, studying the smooth planes and sharp angles of his face in the firelight. His heritage was easy to see in his high cheekbones and the strong contours of his nose. When he turned just so, the flames of the campfire cast blue shadows on his long, thick hair.

He'd never been married. At least Price had never mentioned it in his letters, and Emily wondered now just how John Bandera had managed to escape that particular fate. No man even half as handsome stayed a bachelor well into his thirties in Russell County, even if he was taciturn nearly to the point of rudeness.

How different John Bandera was from Price, she thought, and then immediately felt guilty because she hadn't given the love of her life much thought at all during the last few hours. She hadn't thought of much of anything or anyone except her current companion, and those notions kept taking decidedly physical turns which disconcerted her no end.

It surprised her just how much she wanted this man to like her, how strongly she desired his respect if not affection. Why, she'd even managed to handle his bandaging as if she'd done it a hundred times before, as if the sight of a bare male chest wasn't something wholly new and curiously intriguing for her.

Well, she'd seen her brother, Elliot, of course, but that had been when they were very young. The only other man she'd been close to had been Alvin Gibbons, but their sole union three months ago had been accomplished—and rather clumsily, too— while they were both fully clothed.

The sight of John this evening, stripped of his shirt, had nearly taken her breath away. Touching him as she had, feeling the firm warmth of his flesh and the hard musculature beneath it, had made her stomach do an unexpected, altogether startling flip-flop. Lucky for her it had been dark enough to hide the flush that had crept up from her bodice to her face.

She doubted very much that hers was the first heart that John Bandera had set aflutter, then she found herself wondering about the women in his life. Was he more talkative with them? Did they laugh together? Did he whisper to them in sensuous Spanish?

What would it be like, being kissed by those firm and beautifully sculpted lips? Or touched by those bronzed hands?

Go to sleep right now, Emily ordered herself. *Stop thinking like some brazen tart. You're a well-brought-up young woman even if you are with child. You're not out under the stars with this man because he wants to be here with you. This is all an accident. And, anyway, you foolish thing, you're in love with Price McDaniel.*

She peeked through her lashes one last time at the firelit jaw and the long burnished hair of John Bandera, then promptly cursed herself for giving in to the temptation.

Still, Emily would have given almost anything to know what her flesh-and-blood pillow was thinking as he stared into the dark distance beyond the fire.

Chapter Five

"Just one more mile."

Emily thought those must have been the four sweetest, most beautiful, most welcome words in the English language when John called them over his shoulder to her the next afternoon.

"Oh, good," she answered, trying with all her might to sound as if one more mile was nothing— a pleasant hike, a mere stroll, a promenade—while her feet were in mortal agony and every muscle in her body was clenched in pain. Even the valiant little smiles she tried to fashion every time John glanced in her direction seemed to slice across her face like a cut from a rusty blade.

She refused to complain, though, when she knew her companion was in far worse shape than she was. Not that John had actually said so, but his discomfort was evident from the grim line of his mouth, the squint of his eyes and the rigid set of his shoulders while he walked.

In addition to his battered ribs, he hadn't had so much as a wink of sleep the night before. Emily was certain of this because her own sleep was brief and fitful, and every time she peeked up at her pillow, she discovered him wide-awake, staring into the distance, contemplating she knew not what.

As they trudged back toward The Crippled B, every so often they would come upon a bit of ravaged landscape where yesterday's terrible twister had touched down. Earlier this morning, they had encountered the carcass of a steer. The wind had obviously picked the poor creature up, then dashed him down where one of his long horns stuck deep in the earth while the other pointed forlornly skyward. John had squatted down beside the animal, shaking his head, running a gentle hand over its torn hide.

"Poor devil," he had murmured softly, causing Emily to immediately think of Price and how he had used those same words to describe a longhorn that had gotten bogged down in a puddle one unusually wet spring.

How odd, she thought, that a Southerner of English and Irish extraction, a man raised in a fat-columned mansion with servants and fine silverware and every privilege imaginable, should have so very much in common with this half Comanche who had no roots at all. How strange that two men so different could seem so much alike.

"Sometimes, John, you put me so much in mind of Price," she'd said a little wistfully. "Perhaps it's because the two of you have been together for so long."

But instead of being flattered or even amused by her comment, John had appeared angry. His face grew dark and he practically gnashed his teeth as he stood up, towering over Emily as well as the dead longhorn.

"Maybe we're like twins," he had muttered. "Or like two *solteras*. A couple of old spinsters taking on each other's traits."

After that, he had barely spoken a word to her until the moment he'd announced that they were just one mile from home. Home. The Crippled B.

What if Price had returned home in their absence? Emily wondered all of a sudden.

She looked down at her dirty, limp dress and its tattered hem. She could only guess at the color of her sunburned face and the plight of her windblown hair. Well, Price wouldn't hold that against her, she decided. Hadn't he always written that out here in the West people were judged by what they did, not who they were or what they wore? That was why he preferred it over his birthplace in Mississippi.

She was definitely no longer the pale and prim and properly-turned-out Miss Russell of Russell County, Mississippi. But perhaps Price would be pleased or even proud to judge her as a woman who'd just survived a terrible storm. Two storms, in fact. First there was the twister, and then, more recently, there was John Bandera's most inclement mood.

At the first sight of the ranch house and the out-buildings, John felt like whispering a little prayer of thanks that they all appeared relatively undamaged by the storm. A couple of shingles were missing from the roof and a big branch had been blown from the old live oak tree, but other than that, the place looked reasonably intact.

Unfortunately for him, it looked populated, too. He could just make out the sturdy figure of Señora Fuentes where she stood by the back door tossing handfuls of feed to her prize chickens. Not far away, her daughter, Lupe, with her skirts blowing in the breeze, was pinning wash on the clothesline that ran from the privy to the live oak. So, John thought bleakly, they were back.

He'd almost hoped his housekeeper and her daughter would decide to stay on with their relatives in Nuevo Leon. How the devil was he going to explain Emily to them? He couldn't very well dismiss the pale beauty as a sister or a cousin. Not of his, anyway.

She stood by his side now, one hand lifted to shade her eyes, the other holding back her breeze-blown hair while she stood on tiptoe and strained to see the house.

"Oh," she exclaimed. "There's someone there. Is it…? Do you suppose…?"

It was obvious that her distance vision wasn't as good as his if she held out any hope that it was Price that she was seeing instead of Lupe hanging out the wash. And when he told her so, the disappointment registered only too clearly on her face.

"I thought Price had come back," she said, gazing sadly down at the ground now rather than looking eagerly toward the house.

"No. Not yet," John answered lamely. Not ever, he thought.

"Well, anyway, I'm looking forward to meeting Mrs. Fuentes and her daughter. Price has written me so much about them. I don't know how we'll communicate, though. Neither one of them speaks English, do they?"

"No. No English." Thank God, he thought.

As they slowly neared the house, Señora Fuentes caught sight of them and waved. John could see the woman call out to her daughter then and gesture, with her eloquent chin as well as her expressive hands, in his direction. Lupe squealed—he could hear her even though the wind was blowing and he was still some distance away—and the girl immediately dropped the wet garment in her hand and began running toward him.

Closer to the house, Emily could see better now, and she wondered how she ever could have mistaken this glorious young girl for Price. Lupe was exactly as he had described her from her bare feet and slim brown ankles to her lush bosom and her black hair drawn back in one thick, lustrous braid. She was quite beautiful, Emily thought, and it was obvious that she was more than a little excited to see John. Lupe Fuentes appeared quite delirious, in fact. Somehow in all those letters Price had neglected to mention that the young Mexican woman had such…well…rampant feelings for one of her employers.

Why that caused a sour feeling in Emily's stomach, she couldn't have said. To counter it, however, she put on a wide, welcoming smile.

Lupe didn't slow down at all as she approached them, but rather increased her speed and practically flew at John, wrapping her arms about his neck and her long brown legs about his hips. Then, when he cried out in pain, she quickly untangled herself and stepped back, only to watch the recipient of her enthusiastic greeting sink down on one knee.

"Juanito?" she whispered. The poor girl looked

guilty and baffled, quite stricken in fact, as if she had just caused some terrible accident but had no idea what damage she had wreaked or how she had accomplished it. Then, when it appeared that Lupe was about to reach out to John and attempt to embrace him once more, Emily thrust out a hand to restrain her.

"No. Don't. He's hurt," she told the girl, hoping she'd understand. "Here." Emily pointed to one of her own ribs and grimaced as if in pain.

In spite of the language difference, Lupe seemed to understand because tears suddenly welled in her glossy black eyes. "Oh, *pobrecito,*" she moaned, falling on her knees beside John, pressing a kiss to his shoulder and another to his cheek.

He said something to her in Spanish then, and Lupe responded by standing up, then helping him to his feet.

"What can I do to help, John?" Emily asked.

"Nothing," he said. "Don't worry. I'll be fine after a little rest." He managed a small, tight smile. "You should get a little rest yourself."

He hooked an arm over Lupe's shoulder then and the girl draped her arm carefully about his waist, whispering all the while. Emily followed behind as they made their way to the house. She watched them with more than a little curiosity, intrigued by the physical ease between the two of them, wondering about John's obvious restraint with her when it seemed so easy, so natural for him to touch this young girl and to lean his weight upon her.

Lupe gazed up at him like a moonstruck lover. But for all Emily tried, she couldn't read John's expression when he gazed back.

Mrs. Fuentes showed Emily into one of the two bedrooms upstairs where she discovered her suitcases and steamer trunk, all neatly lined up against a wall. Since John had disappeared into the other bedroom, Emily assumed this must be Price's room, but when she asked, the housekeeper merely smiled politely, shrugged her shoulders and answered in some rapid Spanish that Emily concluded meant the woman did not speak English.

"Price." Emily gestured toward the bed. "Mister...no, I mean, Señor Price McDaniel. This must be his room."

The woman looked at the bed, then back at Emily, bewildered. *"No se, señorita."*

How odd that Mrs. Fuentes didn't even recognize her own employer's name, Emily thought. But, then, perhaps Price was using a Spanish equivalent of his name these days and just hadn't thought to mention it in his letters. If there were a Spanish equivalent of McDaniel, Emily certainly couldn't think of one.

Mrs. Fuentes was patting herself on the stomach now, gazing at Emily with a rather curious smile.

"I... I don't understand," Emily stuttered. Good Lord, it wasn't possible that the woman had discerned her pregnancy in a mere five minutes, was it?

She glanced down at her own stomach to see if it had noticeably grown in the last day or so. It hadn't. She was sure of that. The pleats of her skirt were still just where they should have been, all of them tight and flat across her abdomen.

Then Mrs. Fuentes began to gesture to her mouth while pretending to consume invisible food from her open hand with an equally invisible fork.

"Oh. I see. Now I understand. Am I hungry?" Emily sighed with relief, then nodded eagerly. "Yes, I am. I'm quite famished."

Enormously pleased with herself and with the successful exchange, the housekeeper bustled away, presumably to fix something visible to eat.

Alone then, Emily gazed around the room. Its wallpaper was a light gray with a sober and clearly masculine motif of laurel wreathed medallions. The windows weren't draped, but rather shuttered in a glossy pine which matched the woodwork. Persian rugs were scattered here and there about the room, and in the center of it sat the bed, big and banked at head and foot with intricately carved and curved mahogany. The bed and its matching pieces might very well have come from the McDaniel mansion on Solomon Street. Emily wasn't sure.

But, if this room indeed belonged to Price, she was sure that somebody had emptied it of all his personal effects. She opened a drawer in the night-stand to find it empty. The wardrobe, too, was bare but for two neatly folded wool blankets. Wherever were Price's things? Surely he hadn't taken his entire wardrobe with him on his trip to Abilene.

All she could assume was that, when Mrs. Fuentes had returned from her vacation and spied the luggage in the little room downstairs, the woman had decided to clear out one of her employer's rooms in order to make a proper space for their guest.

Emily sat on the bed and reached out a hand to explore the contours of the mattress where Price had spent so many hours. What would he think when he returned to discover her not only here at The Crippled B, but sleeping in his bed? Would he be angry that she had come west uninvited? Or would he be glad to see her, in spite of what he'd written in that last letter?

Perhaps he had misled her into regarding him as a lover, but certainly not as a friend. And if he was glad to see her, if he continued to be her friend, just how long would that friendship last when she informed him of the child she was going to have?

In all honesty, she couldn't even hope for outright gladness on Price's part. What she hoped for instead was understanding and a portion of the tenderness of which she knew he was capable. If he couldn't return her affection, then she hoped at least to have his blessing and his protection for her child.

Feeling lonely all of a sudden and more than a little anxious about her future, Emily opened the suitcase in which she had so carefully packed her collection of Price's letters. At random she withdrew a ribboned bundle, immediately recognizing the correspondence from two years before, knowing the contents of each envelope by heart.

This one, the third from the bottom with its stamp askew in the corner, contained the sketch Price had done of a giant mesquite tree with its gnarled roots running halfway across the page. The one next to it, she remembered, held the dry and delicate pressed blossom of a bluebonnet between its pages.

She sat back down on the bed with her precious bundle and once again got lost in Price's words, which rang all the more true now that she had seen The Crippled B for herself. So absorbed was she that Emily was barely aware of Mrs. Fuentes when she entered the room with a tray wedged against her ample hip.

This time the housekeeper didn't bother to

speak, but smiled profusely as she placed the tray on the table by the window. Then, when Emily summoned up one of the few words in her meager Spanish vocabulary—*Gracias!*—Mrs. Fuentes nodded enthusiastically and kept nodding even as she went out the door.

Emily practically dived into the plate of scrambled eggs, cooked peppers and buttery tortillas. She had forgotten just how hungry she was, and chuckled at the notion that the prim and proper Miss Russell was not only eating for two now, but eating like a field hand to boot.

Then, after mopping up every bit of butter with her last little triangle of tortilla, she climbed wearily out of her clothes and into Price's bed, where she promptly fell asleep.

Something—a loud voice, a slamming door— awoke her. Emily sat up in bed, astonished by the darkness, not knowing for a moment where she was. Why, she must have slept for hours.

She fumbled on the nightstand, found a match, and lit the lamp. Nine-thirty! That meant she'd slept at least six hours when she'd only planned to close her eyes for a little while before checking on poor John and his injured ribs.

Cursing herself, Emily pawed through her steamer trunk until she found her watered silk wrapper. After that, she searched another piece of luggage for the little box of medicines she had packed. It was a wonder she had thought to bring it at all with her sister-in-law dogging her every step while she packed.

She slipped the vial of laudanum into the pocket of her wrapper and then quietly opened the door to the hallway. If John was asleep, she didn't want to inadvertently wake him. But if he was still awake and in pain, a few drops of her laudanum would soothe him enormously.

Just then the door to his room opened and Lupe stepped out into the hallway.

"Good evening," Emily said, hoping the girl would understand the greeting.

Whether she understood or not, Lupe merely glared at her. Then, without a word, the girl tossed her long raven braid over her shoulder and proceeded to stomp down the stairs as if she meant to break each one.

John's door was ajar, and now Emily nudged it a few more inches. "John? I've brought you some—"

Her voice caught in her throat and so did her breath when she saw him propped on pillows against the headboard, wearing only the bandages on his rib cage and a haphazard quilt that barely covered him from the waist down. The lamp on the dresser burned low, casting a golden sheen over his skin, burnishing his long hair, flickering in the depths of his eyes while he silently met her gaze.

Emily thought she'd never seen anything or anyone quite so beautiful in her life. Beautiful and altogether dangerous. Like some wild thing one wanted to touch but didn't dare. A peculiar warmth stole through her, settling abruptly in the pit of her stomach. She tried to ignore the sensation, and at the same time tried to overcome a sudden and fierce urge to flee.

"I've brought you some laudanum," she said.

He didn't say anything, but merely raised one dark eyebrow.

"Laudanum," she repeated. "Medicine. I thought it might help."

He continued to stare at her as if he didn't understand what she'd said, as if he didn't even recognize her. And only then did it dawn on her that John Bandera was drunk. Dead drunk. He probably *didn't* even recognize her.

She sighed, slipping the vial of laudanum back into the pocket of her wrapper. "I don't suppose you'll be needing this after all. Sleep well, John."

"Emmy."

She had already turned to leave, but now Emily turned back. She could have sworn...

"Come here." He stretched out a hand toward her. "Please."

"No, I... It's very late. And you're..."

"Very drunk." His lips slanted in a lopsided smile and his eyes glittered. "You don't approve?"

Emily shook her head. "I don't disapprove. Under the circumstances, it's probably the best thing you can do."

"Probably," he echoed. "You don't have to be afraid of me."

She stiffened and her chin came up a notch. "That's absurd. I'm not afraid of you."

"Not even a little?"

Emily crossed her arms defensively and snagged her lower lip between her teeth. If she wasn't afraid, why was her heart pounding so? "No, I'm not even a little afraid," she said. "Why would I be?"

He edged up a bit on the pillows now, his mouth thinning in pain as he did. His eyes, though, never left her face. In fact, they had begun to burn into her like two amber flames. "Because you're a very sober lady," he said, "and I'm a very drunk half-breed."

"You're Price's friend and partner, John. I know he respects and trusts you. That means I do, too."

"You trust me?"

"Yes. Of course."

"Then come closer. Come closer to me, Emmy."

Her heart lurched. If he hadn't been so intoxicated, if there hadn't been a distinct slur in his speech, she would have sworn he'd called her by Price's pet name for her.

His hand stretched out to her again and this time it felt as if it was generating some magnetic force, drawing her inevitably to him. Emily took a tentative step forward, toward the bed, but just then the door opened behind her and Lupe stomped in.

"Su botella." She swung the bottle of clear liquid by its neck and her skirts swung about her brown calves when she marched past Emily toward John. She slapped the bottle into his extended hand. *"Toma."*

"Gracias," he said through clenched teeth. Then his gaze slid back to the door, obviously inviting Lupe to use it. *"Vaya."*

"No." The girl's lush lower lip slid out and she bent forward, attempting to smooth out the quilt that covered his legs, leaning to fuss with the pillows behind him.

John pulled the cork from the new bottle with his teeth, then spat it out. *"Vaya,"* he growled.

Lupe snorted and ignored his muttered curses while she continued to fuss over him, stopping only long enough to pitch a dark look toward Emily whom she obviously considered the interloper in his room.

And suddenly, even shamefully, Emily realized she was just that. An interloper. An uninvited guest at a very private affair. She remembered how Lupe had greeted John and how easily they had touched. How naive of her not to have guessed what was going on between John and his housekeeper's daughter. But whatever it was, it was certainly none of Emily's business. She didn't want to know. Anything.

She especially didn't want to know what might have happened if she had taken John's outstretched hand only a moment ago. And if she felt oddly disappointed now, she decided that it was simply because it hadn't been Price who'd called her Emmy and reached out to her.

"Good night," she said, her voice sounding schoolmarmish and as starchy as new muslin.

She closed the door on the lovers and walked back to her own room as quickly as she could. It was difficult not to run.

Chapter Six

When John awoke, he couldn't decide which hurt more—his back or his head. He lay in his bed for a while, gathering enough courage to open his eyes to the sunlight he could feel warming his ankles and feet. *Dios.* He'd drunk enough tequila to last him the rest of his natural life plus several decades in perdition for good measure.

Still with his eyes closed, he took a slow and cautious inventory of his body and came to the conclusion that his rib cage did indeed feel better than his head. The broken rib was probably not broken at all, but only severely bruised and nothing to worry about. What he needed to worry about, though, were the lapses in his memory this morning and the misty visions that floated between those empty spaces.

Visions of beautiful women. Lupe with her dark, demanding eyes, her pouty lips, and her thick, black braid drifting across his chest. Emmy appeared, too, all pale and luminous while hovering in the doorway of his room like a shy, lamplit ghost.

Dear God, what had he done last night? What had he said to her before he'd finally drowned his pain in a river of tequila?

Prying open his eyes, he let them adjust for a moment to the harsh sunlight coming through the window before he tried to focus on anything. The sight of his bare feet brought back a memory of Lupe struggling to pull off his boots while her braid had slanted over her shoulder and the neckline of her thin *camisa* dipped just enough to give him a glimpse of her tawny young breasts.

Now the sight of the rumpled sheets and the quilt twisted about his legs brought a kind of terror to John's heart. *Dios, por favor,* he prayed, tell me it didn't happen. Had he spent the last two years avoiding the young girl's ardent advances only to have succumbed during a drunken stupor?

Another foggy memory solidified then, but this time it wasn't Lupe. It was Emily, wringing her hands, poised for flight in the doorway, saying she wasn't afraid of him. He wondered if he'd told her that she should be afraid, that he couldn't look at her without wanting her, that having her here was more painful than a dozen or more broken ribs. He wondered if, in his tequila haze, he had told her the truth last night. Or if he had lied again, he wondered what new falsehoods he had composed.

He opened his eyes slowly now, allowing the brutal sunshine to seep into his head. Judging from the angle of the sun, it was probably close to noon. He levered up and breathed deeply while the walls ceased their crazy swirling and the floor finally settled into its proper place between them.

Good, he thought. If he'd confessed to Emily last night, then she would hate him this morning and he'd no longer have to contend with her misplaced love for Price. Even if he hadn't told her the truth last night, he'd probably offended her sufficiently to make her keep her distance from him for the duration of her stay at The Crippled B.

Perhaps, John hoped, she was already packing her belongings and preparing to leave, to go back to Mississippi where she belonged. But no sooner had that hope materialized than he heard her Southern voice floating up from the yard below. A voice full of sweet music and invincible good cheer and untrammeled hope.

"Good morning," he heard her say. "I'm Emily Russell, visiting from Mississippi."

Then a less than musical voice replied, "How do, ma'am. I'm Tater Latham, born and bred in Kansas, and I'm awful glad to see another pretty female face around here. Mississippi, huh? Imagine that! You staying long?"

"Well, I really don't know, Mr. Latham. I suppose that depends."

Then, before the biggest, loosest mouth south of the Arkansas River could ask her just what that lengthy stay of hers depended on, John cupped his hands to his mouth and called through the window, "Tater Latham, I want to talk to you. *Right now!*"

The sudden, angry bellow from the window overhead didn't surprise Emily all that much. Whenever her brother had partaken of too much evening whiskey, mornings would always find him loud and irascible, too. John Bandera, as she well knew, had partaken of a great deal of liquor.

And the bellowed command hadn't seemed to surprise Tater Latham, either. The man had merely sighed, tipped his hat to her, then trotted obediently up the steps and into the house.

Emily was sorry to see him go, actually, because she'd been looking forward to a little chat in English after listening to Mrs. Fuentes's Spanish all morning. It seemed to make absolutely no difference to the housekeeper that Emily didn't understand a word she said. The woman just kept talking anyway. The more Emily shrugged and shook her head, the faster and louder Mrs. Fuentes talked.

Lupe was nowhere to be seen, nor was John; Emily imagined the two of them together upstairs. In John's bed. Just why that perturbed her so much, she couldn't have said. It wasn't the impropriety of the affair. Good Lord, who was she to cast stones?

If the young woman's own mother didn't seem concerned with her daughter's carrying on, it really wasn't up to Emily, a perfect stranger, to worry about Lupe. As for John Bandera, he was a grown man and quite capable of making his own choices, including bedmates.

Emily sighed as she stepped off the front porch and began walking toward the corral. Price had often written to her about Smoke, a big, dappled gray stallion he'd purchased in San Antonio the year before and had yet to thoroughly tame. She'd longed to see the magnificent, nearly unbreakable beast, and this morning seemed as good a time as any.

When she reached the corral, a buckskin mare immediately came to the fence, whinnied, and stuck her head out to be petted.

"Good morning, Corazon," Emily said, stroking the horse's long, bony face. "I've heard about you, you old dear. You had a difficult time bringing a colt into the world a few years ago, didn't you?"

The buckskin nodded her head and snuffled softly as if in agreement.

"Poor old thing. Price didn't get any sleep for almost forty-eight hours trying to help you. Then your little foal succumbed after just a few days. It made him very sad. I was so sad for him. And for you.''

She let the mare's soft lips graze her temple and pull gently at her hair while a little ripple of worry ran through her. She'd fretted so much about the social consequences of her pregnancy that she hadn't given much thought to the actual birth itself. It had always seemed so distant, so far in the future, almost unreal. But what if her delivery was as difficult as the mare's? Emily wondered. What if her baby didn't survive? What if she…?

Emily shook her head to banish those grim and morbid thoughts. She was strong and healthy. There was no reason to anticipate the worst. Why, she'd survived a terrible twister, hadn't she?

The mare snuffled softly again. Emily kissed her.

''Next time, Corazon,'' she said, ''I'll bring you a handful of sugar.''

''Don't. It makes her sick.''

Emily turned to find John standing so close behind her that she was in his shadow. Her heart lurched and her hand fluttered up to her throat.

''You frightened me,'' she said.

''Again?'' One of his dark brows lifted. ''Sorry. I tend to walk quietly.''

Emily would have backed up, but she was already against the corral fence. Meanwhile, Corazon took the opportunity to nuzzle her neck, then nudge her forward, smack up against John. There wasn't even time to raise her hands to brace herself before she slammed against his chest with a distinct and breathy *oof.*

John's arms came up automatically to catch her, but letting her go was a different matter after he scented a whiff of rosewater in her golden hair and felt the shape of her waist and the delicate structure of her rib cage beneath his hands. It was a miracle, he thought, that he hadn't killed this fragile woman the other day when he'd thrown his weight on top of her to shield her from the storm.

He closed his eyes to block out everything but her, savoring his Emmy in his arms, treasuring this moment, wishing it could last forever.

"Sure hope ol' green-eyed Lupe don't catch you like that, Boss. She'll have your hide and then some," Tater Latham drawled from somewhere behind him, then snickered as he passed by on his way to the barn.

The cowboy might just as well have doused them with a bucket of cold water. Emily made a kind of sputtering noise and pulled back. She stared at the ground, her hands fidgeting with the folds of her skirt.

"I'm very sorry, John."

"Sorry? For what?"

"Well, I wouldn't want to be responsible for getting you in trouble."

"Trouble?"

Her blue eyes lifted to his for a second. "With Lupe, of course."

"With…?"

He started to laugh, but stopped when he thought better of it. It could only be good if Emily thought that he and Lupe were lovers. He ought to welcome any barriers between himself and this woman. Her mistaken notion of his involvement with Lupe would help keep some distance between them, and John needed all the distance he could get. His self-control was thin as ice on a November pond, and every time Emily looked at him or stood close, that control melted a little bit more.

He stepped back another foot, then tried to smile the way a lover would when discussing his mate.

"It's not your problem. Sometimes young Lupe's a little too possessive. She tends to see trouble where it doesn't exist."

Emily gave a mournful little laugh. "I suppose I should be flattered, being taken for a rival by such a beautiful young girl."

He shrugged rather than tell her she was the most beautiful woman he knew, the most beautiful woman that he could ever hope to know, and he watched her lips lose an inaudible sigh before she turned back to gaze into the corral and idly stroke Corazon's nose.

"Perhaps I should leave," she said as much to the horse as to John.

Yes, that would solve all his problems. No, that would kill him.

"What? Go back to Mississippi?" he asked.

She laughed softly at that, leaning her head against Corazon's muzzle. "No. Not Mississippi. Not quite that far. I was thinking of taking a room in Santander. Isn't that the closest town?"

"Yes. It's a two-hour ride."

"It might be days, even weeks, before Price returns. I don't want to be a burden here or a source of discontent between you and Lupe."

John was silent. It was distance he craved, wasn't it? He ought to be glad she was taking it upon herself to leave. He ought to be throwing his hat a mile high in the air and cheering instead of feeling as if he'd just been kicked in the stomach.

"Well, then." Emily sounded decisive as she turned back toward him. "Will you arrange for someone to take me there, John? To Santander. Tomorrow, if possible."

"I'll arrange it."

But he already knew who would take her and just how much the bittersweet journey would cost him.

*   *   *

Santander wasn't much more than a watering hole for men bringing cattle up from Mexico. It had a population of a hundred souls, give or take a soul or two, one mercantile, one livery, one saloon, one little adobe church which the priest visited on alternate Sundays and one dilapidated Baptist shack which hadn't seen a real preacher in three years.

So quiet and sleepy was the village that, when John's wagon came down the dusty, sun-baked street, the chickens and pigs merely sidestepped to get out of its way.

"You'll be safe here," he said, pulling the wagon up in front of the saloon. "Hy Slocum and his wife rent out a couple rooms above the saloon, and they don't tolerate any shady business. You won't have to worry about anything."

"I wasn't worried." Emily closed her parasol. "You've taken good care of me, John. I'm grateful, and I know that Price will be, too, when he returns."

John gritted his teeth while he set the brake. He thought if he heard one more reference to the absent, the invisible, the probably late and wholly unlamented Price McDaniel, his head might just explode. His heart, by now, was fairly numbed to Emily's references.

"Wait here," he told her, "while I make sure the Slocums have a room."

What he wanted to make sure of was that Hy kept his mouth closed about Price, who had spent more than a few nights in the rooms upstairs after his drunken binges. He didn't have to worry about Sarah's saying anything since Price was already gone by the time she arrived in Santander two years ago and slipped her wedding noose good and tight around Hy's bald head.

As usual, when the place was empty, the barkeep was sitting at one of the tables, lost in a game of solitaire. John could almost see his own reflection in Hy's glossy pate. It never failed to amaze him that a man could have so much hair on his upper lip and not a single one on his head.

"You winning?" John asked, pulling out a chair across from Hy, then straddling it and leaning his arms on its spooled back.

Hy Slocum raised his head and grinned. "Damn, John. I haven't seen your half-breed hide in months. How've you been?"

"Pretty good. How's business?"

"How's it look?" Hy scowled, then moved a red nine on a black ten. "Now that Sarah's here, all my dependable drunks have gone elsewhere." He laughed a little mournfully. "You're my first customer today. *El numero uno,* John. I got a keg of fine lager from Saint Louis last week. Want a sample?"

John shook his head. "No, thanks. I've got a lady waiting outside. She's looking for a room."

"Oh, yeah? Well, go on and bring her in. Sarah's got both rooms all tidied up and ready. Lord knows she'll be glad as cake to have a little female company, too. Lemme just go out back and give her a shout."

Hy put down his cards and started to get up, but John stopped him.

"Just one thing before I bring the lady in." He lowered his voice a conspiratorial notch and hoped to hell he remembered the story he'd rehearsed. "This woman's a relative of Price's, Hy, and came out here looking for him, but I haven't been able to work up the courage to tell her he's probably dead. The lady's in a sort of delicate way, and…"

"You mean she's gonna have a baby?"

John laughed at the absurdity of the question. "No. Not hardly. She's a single lady. Real proper. It's just that, well, she's had a lot of bad luck lately and one more piece of unfortunate news might be her undoing."

Hy nodded sympathetically. "Some women are like that. Real fragile."

"She's that, all right. So I'd appreciate it, Hy, when she starts asking questions about Price, if you'd just tell her you don't know him."

"Well, that won't be all that hard to do, will it?" the barkeep said. "I mean, I hardly did know him, did I? McDaniel never did talk much when he was in here. He just drank.''

John nodded in agreement. ''Much obliged, Hy. I'll go get Miss Russell now. She's waiting outside.''

Emily was peering over the side of the wagon, watching a bristle-backed pig as it snuffled and dug at the front wheel, hoping the confounded animal wouldn't spook the horses. Then somebody hissed and yelled, ''Go on now, you pig. Get.'' The pig snorted indignantly, then trotted away.

''You must be waiting on John,'' the same voice proclaimed. ''Pleased to meet you. I'm Sarah Slocum.''

Now Emily found herself looking down at a pretty redhead in a yellow calico dress. The woman's plump cheeks were flushed and from the snugness of her bodice and the fullness of the gathers on her skirt, it was obvious that she was heavy with child.

''I'm Emily Russell. And, yes, I am waiting on John. He's in there—'' she nodded toward the saloon ''—seeing about a room.''

''For you?''

''Yes.''

The redhead's smile increased and her eyes sparkled. ''Well, how about that! So you're the one.''

''The one?''

"The one he's been pledged to for all these years. I was beginning to think you were just some story he'd made up to keep all his admirers at a distance."

"I'm not..."

Sarah Slocum was laughing now, not listening. "I'll be damned. It was true all along. That big, handsome son of a Comanche gun was telling the truth. So, when's the wedding?"

"Oh, no. There's no..."

John appeared in the doorway of the saloon just then, attracting Sarah Slocum's attention like a six-foot-two-inch magnet.

"You devil, John Bandera," she exclaimed. "And here I thought you were making up all those stories about your intended."

A grin slashed across his face as he came toward the wagon. "Looks like you're making up something yourself, Mrs. Slocum," he said, eyeing her blooming abdomen. "Hy didn't say a word about a little one coming along."

She laughed. "That's 'cause he's scared to death. You'd think he was the one planning to give birth."

Emily watched while John put a big, bronzed hand on each of Sarah's shoulders, then kissed the top of her head. Once more, she marveled at the ease he seemed to feel with women. Lupe. Sarah Slocum. The mysterious woman to whom he was pledged. Everyone but her. It made sense, she supposed. It was only natural that John would be restrained, even somewhat cool with his partner's longtime love. But still…

When he came around to her side of the wagon and stood there, arms outstretched to help her down, Emily imagined for just a moment that John was being more than polite, that he meant to embrace her rather than merely guide her to the ground.

"Ready?" he asked.

"Yes."

She closed her eyes when his fingers curled around her waist, then she breathed in the warm, leathery scent of him as he lifted her down. Even after her feet were firmly planted on the street, she leaned against him a moment or two, absorbing his solidity and his strength.

"Motherhood looks good on you," he said.

Emily's eyes flew open and she straightened up. "I beg your pardon?" It was only then that she realized, much to her embarrassment, that John was still talking to Sarah, who stood on the opposite side of the wagon.

Sarah laughed again. "Motherhood will look a whole lot better once this baby's in my arms instead of kicking the daylights out of my insides." She aimed a knowing glance at Emily. "You'll see just what I mean one of these days. Come on. John, you get your lady's luggage and I'll make sure the room's all ready for her.''

When the redhead disappeared through the saloon door, John said quietly, ''I guess Sarah thinks you're somebody else.''

''Yes, I gathered that.'' Emily cocked her head. ''Who?''

''Just somebody.'' He lifted her steamer trunk from the back of the wagon and gathered up all the other luggage.

''That's all of them. Let's go.''

With her curiosity running rampant now, Emily didn't budge. ''Who, John?'' she asked. ''Who did Sarah mistake me for?''

Halfway to the saloon door, he stopped and turned to her. His expression was somber now, almost tragic. Every line in his rugged face seemed deeper. The light in his amber eyes had dimmed. He seemed to have aged a decade or more in the last ten seconds. It was all Emily could do not to rush to him.

''A woman I used to love,'' he said. ''It's not important.''

''A woman you *still* love,'' she corrected gently. ''I can see it clearly on your face.''

''Maybe.'' He shrugged. ''It doesn't matter.''

''Oh, John. You couldn't be more wrong. Love matters. It matters more than anything else. Why, look at me. I've come hundreds of miles, all for the sake of love.''

"You shouldn't have," he said brusquely. Then he turned his back on her and strode through the door.

He might as well have slapped her across the face for all his words stung. They hadn't discussed her relationship with Price at any length, but Emily had never gotten the impression that John disapproved. Suddenly she felt as if he not only disapproved, but could barely stand the sight of her. She felt like an intruder again.

Well, she wasn't. Dammit. What did John Bandera know of all the intimacies that she and Price had shared in their correspondence? What did he know about love at all when he so casually disregarded a woman who'd meant so much to him in the past? And what about poor Lupe? How dare this man, this little more than a stranger, tell her she shouldn't have come to Texas when it was the best and bravest thing she'd ever done in her entire life?

She gathered her skirts in both fists, about to stalk after John and give him a good piece of her mind, when all of a sudden there was strange movement inside her, like a butterfly beating its wings.

Her child!

Emily stood there a moment, absolutely still,

stupefied by the quickening, longing desperately for Price's return so he could share this miracle of miracles with her. Her anger at John Bandera dissolved.

Let him think what he wanted. It didn't matter. Let John approve or disapprove of her. Either way, she didn't care. John wasn't Price, after all.

Chapter Seven

The women were upstairs, more than likely talking their pretty heads off while inspecting the room. Downstairs, in the saloon, John had accepted Hy Slocum's offer of the newly arrived Saint Louis beer.

He didn't feel right about leaving Emily without a proper goodbye, especially after his cruel remark about the miles she'd come for the sake of love. She figured him for an insensitive brute now. He knew because she'd hissed those words, among others, in his direction before she went upstairs.

Well, hell, he supposed he was an insensitive brute, but he didn't know what else he could be under the circumstances. He should have never written that first letter six years ago. Then Emily would never have fallen in love with Price—with him! She'd have been free to love a proper gentleman in Russell County, marry him, and even have two or three babies by now.

Instead, no thanks to John, here she was—twenty-six years old, childless, and completely devoted to a lover made of paper and ink. He'd ruined her life, John thought bleakly. It went without saying that he'd ruined his own.

He sat watching the barkeep cheat at solitaire, wondering whether it was because Hy liked to win or just plain hated to lose. Probably a little bit of both, he decided.

"Congratulations on the kid," John said, tilting his beer glass across the table in a casual toast to the future father.

Hy's mouth tightened a bit beneath his thick mustache. "Thanks. Sarah looks good, doesn't she? She's happy enough about it."

"And you're not?"

"Oh, I'm happy, I guess. It'll be nice to have a little one around here. Who knows? Maybe he'll look like me."

John laughed. "Bald as an onion, you mean. I expect he will."

"Yeah." Hy studied the cards on the tabletop a moment, then swore softly as he gathered them into a pile. "Played out, dammit."

"Sarah will be fine. Hell, women have been having babies since the beginning of time, Hy. Don't worry so much."

"That's what I keep telling him," Sarah said brightly as she approached the table. "From the way Hy keeps carrying on, you'd all but think I was the first woman to ever do this."

She bent to kiss her husband's smooth, shiny head, then winked at John. "Your lady friend's getting settled in upstairs. What in the world did you say to her, John, to get her so riled?"

John drained his glass, then sighed as he pushed back from the table and stood up. "Hard telling," he muttered as if he didn't know the reason. "Whatever it was, though, I guess I'd better get myself upstairs and see about an apology."

"It's the first door on the right," Sarah said. There was a twinkle in her eye when she added, "You just take your sweet, slow time with that apology, too, John Bandera, if you know what I mean."

He knew exactly what she meant, and for a moment John devoutly wished he were going upstairs to make those sweet and slow amends to his Emmy rather than to bid her a bitter and brief farewell.

Emily was standing at the room's only window, staring out at somebody's limp union suit pinned to a clothesline, wondering if it was Hy Slocum's and whether or not Sarah took delight in the laundering and mending of such intimate apparel.

She would have, she thought. Not that she'd

ever washed anything more than a hankie in her life, but just then, a handful of wet, soapy men's underclothes or a dozen diapers boiling in a big pot struck her as far more precious and more desirable than anything in the world. How eager she was to begin the brand-new life that the West promised. How she longed for that. And how sad that she was here, alone, in a rented room. It was little more than limbo.

She pictured the laundry line at The Crippled B suddenly, and herself instead of Lupe standing on tiptoe, pinning wet garments to the taut rope. When was her life going to begin?

There was a soft knock on her door.

"Come in," Emily called, glad for the interruption to her mournful thoughts and anticipating another pleasant chat with Sarah Slocum. When she turned from the window, though, it wasn't Sarah who was standing there, but John Bandera, hat in hand, his broad shoulders measuring the width of the doorway. Her heart—that damnably disruptive thing somewhere inside her chest—performed a tiny, perfect, head-over-heels somersault at the mere sight of him.

"You should be getting back to the ranch, shouldn't you?" she inquired coolly, ignoring the beat of her heart but crossing her arms high, anyway, just in case that wild beat was visible.

"Soon," he said, stepping decisively into the

room and pulling the door closed behind him. "Look. About what I said earlier…"

Emily clenched her teeth. She should have known the insensitive brute wouldn't be content until he'd argued her into submission. Every man she'd ever encountered was that way. Pigheaded. Prideful. Unwilling to be wrong. They were all the same. Well…with the singular, shining exception of Price.

"Let's just forget it, please. You're entitled to your opinion, Mr. Bandera. You needn't explain." She turned back to the window. "I'd prefer not to discuss my personal affairs with you."

John sighed. So he was Mr. Bandera, again, was he?

Well, fine. She wasn't the only one riled now. How could Emmy have been so foolish, coming hundreds of miles for nothing, for no one? He wanted to shake her.

"Seems to me your personal affairs don't exist at the moment, Miss Russell."

Her back stiffened. Her voice climbed half an octave. "Which is, once again, your way of saying I shouldn't have come here, I presume."

"Presume this, lady," he growled. "What if your ever-lovin' Price just doesn't happen to come back from Abilene? Ever?"

She whirled around and stared at him now, her face a shade or two paler than it had been only a moment before, her eyes a good deal wider and dramatically darker. "What do you mean?"

Dios! What the hell did he mean? John asked himself. He'd come upstairs a minute ago to say an honest, even a heartfelt goodbye and now here he was, jealous of a dead man, jealous of himself— *Madre de Dios!*—and, if that wasn't bad enough, he was lying like some slit-eyed snake oil peddler. Again!

"I mean, goddammit, I don't know what my partner is up to these days or why he's stayed in Kansas all this time. How should I know? Maybe he's found himself a woman up there."

"Maybe he's ill," she countered hotly.

"Maybe you shouldn't put so much damned faith in a man you don't know all that well, lady."

"Maybe you should leave, Mr. Bandera." Her hands fisted on her hips and her chin shot out sharply. "Right now."

"Fine."

John slapped his hat against his leg, then jammed it onto his head. "You take care of yourself, Miss Russell. Enjoy your stay in Santander. When and if Price ever does decide to come back, I'll be sure and let him know where he can find you."

"I'd appreciate that," she said stiffly.

He headed for the door, then stopped. "Just how

long are you planning to wait for him, anyway?''

"As long as it takes," she answered.

"As long as it takes," John muttered to himself for the hundredth time. "As long as it confounded, damn blasted takes."

He'd been talking to himself like some crazy man—*un hombre demente*—for the past hour on his way back to The Crippled B. Even the horses had begun casting wary glances back at their lone but loquacious driver.

He'd spent his thirty-four years being direct and honest and fearless of the consequences of both his actions and his speech. He was proud of that, dammit. It was the way a man should be. But now he was nothing better than a lying coward who could hardly stand to meet his own gaze in a shaving mirror. And not only was he lying to Emily, but asking others—Tater Latham and Hy Slocum, for instance—to lie to her, as well.

He pulled back hard on the reins and sat there, staring into the distance, seeing nothing, thinking how it had all gone so badly wrong and how he didn't have a clue how to fix it. There was the truth, of course, but whoever said *The truth shall set you free* must've been an honest-to-God fool or else had never loved a woman the way that John loved Emmy.

The truth wouldn't make her free. It would make her feel cheated and deceived, played the fool by

a mongrel of a man who didn't belong in her ped-
igreed world. She'd despise him for all time.

Well, he deserved it, John thought. Maybe that
was the answer. Maybe that was only thing he
could give her by way of reparations. Then she
wouldn't be empty forever the way he was planning to be. She would be filled with hate, instead.

Yes, that's just what he'd do, by God. He would
gift his Emmy with the truth and, along with it, a
fearsome, all-consuming hate to replace the love
she bore for a man who didn't exist.

He flicked the reins, pulling hard on the left,
turning the wagon back toward town.

There wasn't much to do in Santander. That had
become all too obvious to Emily once she'd made
a circuit of the dusty, dismal little town, accom-
panied partway by a brindled piglet who appeared
equally unemployed. Ten minutes after stepping
outside the Slocums' saloon, she was back at the
door again, dreading the return to her stifling hot
room on the second floor.

There was a rectangle of shade beneath the saloon's narrow corrugated porch roof, so she sat
there awhile, fanning herself and watching an occasional brave soul cross the sun-baked street from
one building to another before disappearing again.
She'd told John that she'd wait here as long as it
took for Price to return, but now the prospect of

spending anything over a few days in this place seemed utterly and unbearably depressing.

Thankfully, Sarah Slocum stepped outside just then, and as if she'd somehow read Emily's mind, the woman sighed and said, ''This town's about as lively as a graveyard, I'm afraid.''

Emily laughed in response. ''I was just thinking the same thing myself. Is it always like this?''

''Pretty much.'' Sarah lowered herself a bit awkwardly onto the bench beside her. She gestured toward the livery, where a pig was trying to claim a piece of shade under a broken-down buckboard. ''More pigs than people,'' she said with a snort. ''You'd have been a lot better off staying at The Crippled B with John Bandera, married or not. It's different from where you came from in Mississippi. Believe me, there's nobody around here gives three hoots for proprieties like that.''

''Well, it wasn't exactly that,'' Emily said.

''John's a good man, Miss Russell. Hardworking. Faithful. You're a lucky woman.''

''That may be, but I...''

Emily didn't know just how to explain about Price and their correspondence without making herself sound foolish, but as it happened Sarah wasn't listening anyway. Her attention was currently focused on three men riding into town from the east.

''Speaking of pigs,'' Sarah muttered. She lugged

herself to her feet. "Those boys from the Bettman ranch won't do you any harm, so don't be put off if they say something crude. They're good customers, but not one of them knows the first thing about how to treat a lady, if you know what I mean."

She called through the door into the saloon then. "Hy, get your tap hand working. Rudy and Pete and Walleye are here."

"Perhaps I'll go up to my room," Emily said, watching the three men guide their mounts down the middle of the street, churning a tan cloud of dust in their wake and scattering chickens and pigs as they came.

"If you want," Sarah said. "Like I said, they're just playful. Don't feel you have to run and hide, though. You're safe enough with me and Hy."

Emily didn't feel all that safe seeing three leering pairs of eyes locked on her now from a distance of a few hundred feet. Back home most of her encounters with the male sex had been closely chaperoned. Well, with the exception of her disastrous encounter with Alvin a few months ago. She stood up, preparing to retreat upstairs just as the three men drew their horses up at the hitching rail.

"Here now," one of them called out. "Hold on, little lady. Where're you rushing off to?"

Sarah gave a snort. "She is a lady, Rudy, so you

just keep that in mind while you're keeping your hands off of her, you hear?''

The barrel-chested cowboy named Rudy tugged on his earlobe and grinned. ''What's that you say, Sarah? Would I mind doing what with my hands?''

''You heard me,'' she replied. ''Miss Russell here is pledged to John Bandera.''

Rudy stopped grinning.

''Yeah,'' Sarah said. ''I thought that information would take a little polish out of that smile of yours.'' She grabbed up her skirts and turned to go inside. ''Hy's got a fresh keg of beer, fellas. Come on in.''

Emily began to follow, but a hand clamped around her elbow.

''Now, just a minute, darlin'. What's a nice lady like you doing keeping company with a durned half-breed like Bandera? You from around here, sis?''

Emily looked up into the unshaven face of the man she assumed was called Walleye, wondering how he could even see her when one of his eyes gazed due east and the other went off vaguely southwest. His grin was as crooked as his gaze. So were his teeth.

''I'm from Mississippi,'' she said, jerking her arm from his grasp, ''where gentlemen don't accost ladies on the street.''

Walleye laughed. ''Well, you're not in Mississippi now, sis. You're in Texas. And I ain't no gentleman. Leastways, not the last time I looked.''

The third cowboy, Pete, hooted with laughter at the hitching rail and called out, "Last time you looked, Walleye, you probably thought you was two gentlemen." He looped his reins over the rail. "Leave her be, boys. We came here to wet our whistles, not our peckers."

"Speak for yourself, Pete," Walleye grumbled. "And when's the last time you saw a lady sitting outside a saloon? Huh?" He curled his fingers around Emily's arm again. "Thirsty, are you? What're you waiting out here for, sis? Somebody to buy you a couple of beers and then take you on upstairs?"

"The lady's waiting for me."

John Bandera stepped out of the saloon door. His face was dark as a storm and his voice was deeper than thunder.

"Let go of her, Walleye, if you want to keep that hand."

Where he'd come from, Emily didn't have a clue, but she knew she'd never been so glad to see anybody in her entire life. She knew, too, that she'd never seen anybody who looked even half as dangerous as John did now with his lips pulled back in a snarl and the bronze cords on his neck straining quite visibly. Beside her, she heard Walleye swallow hard, and when his grip on her arm slackened, she pulled away.

"Aw, hell. He was only fooling," Pete said as he angled himself between the two men. "Where's your sense of humor, Bandera?"

"I never had one." John moved closer to Emily and curved his arm around her waist. "This lady belongs to me. Anybody got a problem with that?"

"Not if she don't," Walleye muttered, his errant gaze looking more sheepish than wolfish now.

"The only problem I've got is thirst," Pete said, giving Walleye a little shove toward the door. "Let's go get that beer."

After the cowboys had traipsed inside the saloon, John's arm remained firmly about Emily's waist. A quick glance up at his face revealed a fierce anger that hadn't yet subsided as he stared toward the barroom door.

"Well, that was unpleasant," she said, trying to sound as if the incident hadn't terrified her, as if she had successfully fended off scores of such ruffians in the past. "Thank you very much, John. I'm very grateful for your intervention."

"The wagon's out back. Wait there while I get your things."

Emily stepped away, blinking. "But I've only just arrived."

"And now you're leaving."

She stiffened. He was using the very same tone

with her that he had used only a moment before with the three cowboys. Harsh. Unyielding. Daring her to disagree. And, oddly enough, even though Emily resented his domineering stance, she was suddenly and outrageously grateful to be returning to the relative safety of The Crippled B.

"All right," she answered with all the calmness and good grace she could muster, as if the return trip had been her idea in the first place. "I'll just go in and say a quick goodbye to Sarah."

"You'll wait in the wagon," he told her. "I'll send Sarah out."

"But I…"

He swore roughly in Spanish just before he caught her shoulders in a fearsome grip. "You'll wait for me in the wagon, or we'll leave right now. No luggage. No goodbyes. No nothing. *Nada.* It's up to you."

"But I merely—"

"Silencio!"

He shook her then, hard enough for her hair to come loose from its ribbon and her teeth to fairly rattle in her head. If John had appeared enraged earlier, he looked nearly savage now.

"Listen to me, for the love of God. Get in the wagon, Emily. Do it now. Don't make me kill a man today just because you're beautiful."

Chapter Eight

"**Y**ou really meant it, didn't you, John?" Emily asked out of the silent blue. "You meant what you said back there about killing that man."

They were three miles west of Santander. A threesome, John was thinking. Himself, Emily, and the silence that sat heavily between them. Her sudden question may have surprised him, but not its subject.

The woman he knew so well abhorred violence in even its smallest form. She'd written him so often about that over the years. He remembered her telling him that she once wrapped a spider in a handkerchief and carried it safely outdoors rather than swat it or step on it.

When she was ten or eleven years old, she had rescued a baby squirrel from the jaws of a hound, then bandaged it and nursed it back to health only to be bitten herself and abandoned when the little ingrate took to the wild again. She had named the squirrel Caesar Augustus, Gus for short. But, of course, since John wasn't Price, he wasn't supposed to know that.

And since he wasn't the genteel Price, but a savage half-breed in her opinion, his threat to do violence back in Santander had probably come as no surprise. He wondered how she'd managed to disguise the disapproval in her voice and the disdain from her expression.

"This is Texas," he said in response to her question. "Things have a way of escalating out here. They get out of hand. Men do."

She glanced at him briefly, almost shyly. "Including you?"

"Including me," he said. "I'm no different from anybody else."

She gave him an odd look then, made all the more inscrutable by the smallest wisp of a smile. If he hadn't known better, John would've thought she was flirting with him. At any rate, something he'd said or done seemed to amuse her no end.

"What?" he asked her. "Why are you smiling?"

"You came back this afternoon."

"Yeah."

Now she tilted her head a little, and that confounded smile tilted, too. "Why?"

"Why'd I come back?" It wasn't that he didn't

understand the question. He simply didn't know the answer anymore. At least not the one he was prepared to give her. So much for the brave, unvarnished truth, he thought bleakly. The only thing worse than a coward was a lovestruck coward.

And then, before he even realized he was speaking, a kind of truth came out.

"I wanted to see you again," he said.

"Oh." The word came forth with a tiny gulp.

He couldn't tell if Emily was shocked or appalled or if she'd just swallowed a fly. And after that surprised little exclamation, she didn't say another word, but merely sat there, staring straight ahead when she wasn't fussing with the strings of her handbag or the seams of her gloves or the lace at the end of her sleeves.

Her reaction was about what John had expected, not to mention what he deserved. Probably, he thought, she was just too polite and much too tenderhearted to tell him that, although she was flattered by his admission and very grateful that he had returned to scare off those three randy cowboys, she simply wasn't interested in the attentions of someone—some bastard son of a Comanche woman—like him. How could she be?

Once again, silence took up a dark, impenetrable space between them.

It seemed as if they'd been traveling for hours, so Emily assumed they must be getting close to the ranch house by now. She'd been silent so long that she thought her voice would come out sounding like a dry and shriveled croak if she tried to speak. Her silence alone was traitorous enough.

I wanted to see you again.

John wanted to see her again!

She told herself she should have spoken out and discouraged him immediately. She should have laughed gaily, a belle of the ball only too accustomed to such attentions, treating them all as mere trifles. *Oh, John, you say the sweetest things.* Or she should have been strict and stern, staring him down and lashing him with her indignation.

I'll just pretend I didn't hear that, John, she should have said. *And I'll thank you to remain silent on this subject in the future. Need I remind you, sir, that I'm pledged to your partner?*

Only she wasn't indignant. Surprised, yes. And quite taken aback. Even secretly thrilled by his declaration. God forgive her, but she'd wanted to see him again, too. The moment John had stormed out of her little room above the saloon in Santander, she'd wished that he'd come storming back.

Stealing a glance at his strong bronzed hands on the reins, Emily guiltily imagined her own pale fingers entwined with his, and she found herself wishing once more to touch his warm flesh the way she had the night she'd torn up her petticoats and bound his injured ribs. A heat that had nothing to do with Texas sunshine crept up her neck and spread across her face. Her heart felt quite odd, both empty and full at once.

Never before had she felt a purely physical attraction for a man. For dark, strong hands and ropy forearms and muscles enticingly veiled and hardly disguised by chambray and wool. For the deep, exotic resonance of a Spanish-accented voice. For the scents of plain soap and hard work. The creak of a leather belt, the clank of a metal buckle, the music of spurs.

Since she barely knew John Bandera, the attraction couldn't have been anything other than physical, but its sheer power astonished her. It felt like a living thing, curling in the pit of her stomach, regulating the beat of her heart, making her blood run hotter. In contrast, her feelings for Price seemed pale and ethereal, born of a spiritual bond that had nothing at all to do with the pleasures or temptations of the flesh.

She wondered if her feelings had something to do with the fact that she had lost her innocence. Now that she was a fallen woman, would she be susceptible to these physical desires that had never moved her before? Wanton once, wanton always? Was that her fate?

As they neared The Crippled B, it suddenly occurred to Emily that if Price were there—back from Abilene—standing on the porch to welcome them, her first reaction would be one of disappointment. Disappointment! At seeing Price, her dearest Price, whom she'd longed to see for six long years! How could she possibly feel that way?

And then, as if the fates truly meant to taunt or punish her, the ranch house did come into view, and there was someone—a tall, lean, fair-haired someone—standing on the porch. Dear Lord, it couldn't be, could it? Emily leaned forward, squinting hard, trying with all her might to bring the man's features into focus.

''Price?'' His name was a whisper, barely more than a cool shiver across her lips.

Beside her, John said nothing, but he suddenly sat up straighter and his dark hands twitched on the reins to make the horses pick up speed.

Whoever the hell the stranger was, he came down the front steps and advanced on the wagon like a man bent on making trouble.

John shifted on the seat, the better to access his pistol if he had to. The stranger wasn't wearing a gun, but you never knew with fancy dressers like him. There might be a one-shot concealed up the sleeve of his frock coat or a dagger inside the shank of one of his high, glossy boots. Armed or not, the man looked red-faced and wild-eyed with anger, and that alone was enough to make him dangerous.

He shook a fist as he came toward the wagon. "Emily Russell, you ought to be ashamed for what you've put us through. Damn you. I ought to throttle you, you foolish, thoughtless creature."

John hauled back on the reins and held them securely. The irate son of a bitch was sputtering and flapping both of his arms now, pinwheeling and spitting wildly enough to spook the horses.

"Where the devil have you been, Emily Russell?" the man shouted at the top of his lungs. "And who the devil is this?" He stabbed a finger toward John. "It certainly isn't Price McDaniel."

"Elliot!" Emily exclaimed.

"Do you know this character?" John asked her, without taking his eyes off the character in question.

"Indeed I do," she answered a little breathlessly. "This character happens to be my brother."

"Your…"

"Her brother, her guardian and her confounded keeper," Elliot Russell shouted. He widened his stance and crossed his arms over his chest, all the while glaring at John. "Now, if you don't mind, I'd like to know just who the devil you are, sir."

The *sir* was uttered more as an insult than a polite form of address, so John was equally civil when he replied, "This is my land and that's my house."

"He's John Bandera, Elliot. Price McDaniel's partner," Emily interjected. "And he's my kind host, I might add. How dare you show up here behaving so rudely and insufferably?"

John thought he could see the family resemblance now, at least as far as temperament was concerned. The brother was shaking his fist again and Emily was poking her parasol practically in his face. The horses, meanwhile, were becoming loose-footed and wild-eyed, snorting and blowing as they tried to identify the danger and decide whether to bolt or rear back in their traces.

"Help your sister down, mister, before this team runs us halfway to the next county," he ordered Russell. "And you," he said to Emily, "put that blasted umbrella away before you poke somebody's eye out."

"If I do, it certainly won't be an accident," she muttered under her breath. "You know why he's here, don't you, John? My brother's come to drag me back to Mississippi."

"There's not going to be any dragging, Emily," John said calmly. "Not unless it's these horses. Get down now. Go on."

Grudgingly and muttering all the while, she allowed her brother to help her to the ground. Once down, she parried her parasol like a sword, fending him away.

John sighed mightily as he guided the skittish horses around the two combatants and headed the wagon to the barn where Tater Latham stood chuckling as he leaned just inside the door.

"You know, boss, if General Lee had had himself a couple brigades of ladies with lethal umbrellas like that, he mightn't have lost the war," Tater said, nodding toward the commotion near the front porch. "What's all the confounded fuss?"

"Damned if I know. See to these animals, will you, Tater?" John climbed down from the wagon. "How long's that fella been here?"

"Since about noon. The mud wagon from Corpus Christi delivered him, and he's been stomping around in those fancy boots of his ever since, yelling at poor ol' Señora Fuentes when she can't understand a single word he's saying, then coming out here and asking me all kinds of questions."

John frowned. "What kind of questions?"

"He started out asking the whereabouts of Miss Russell, and when I couldn't give him a satisfactory answer, he started asking about McDaniel."

John felt the ground shift imperceptibly under his feet. He was used to being in control of events, and now they seemed to be spinning out of his reach. "What did you tell him?"

"About McDaniel?" Tater laughed and nudged

his hat back on his head. "Nothing. By then that little Southern banty cock had me so hot under the collar that I wouldn't even have given him the time of day if he'd offered me a hundred dollars for it."

"Good," John said. The earth felt a bit more solid beneath him. He was still in control. For the moment, anyway.

"Just stay out of his way, Tater. I'll handle him. In fact, I want you to ride out to the line shack on the Arroyo Roja and see if any repair work needs to be done. That twister the other day probably did a pretty fair amount of damage."

"Sure, boss. Glad to. I'll saddle up right now." Tater angled his head toward the house. "Believe you me, I don't mind missing out on these festivities one little bit."

"I wouldn't mind missing them myself. When you're done with the horses, Tater, see that Miss Russell's bags get into the house, will you?" Then, with a sigh, John exited the barn and walked toward the house where the sister-brother altercation continued, hot and heavy, on the porch.

Maybe he should be glad, he thought, that Russell had come to take Emily home. The man obviously had his sister's welfare at heart. He'd come a far distance to prove that, even if he did behave more like a fighting cock than a concerned sibling. Why the hell hadn't he kept her home in the first place? John wondered. That would have solved everybody's problems.

He gazed across the dusty, hoof-trodden grass that amounted to his front yard. The Russells, brother and sister, were still on the porch. Emily had abandoned her parasol for her two expressive hands and a stance akin to a lightweight pugilist. Elliot was stalking back and forth, wearing an angry groove in the porchboards while his fists punched holes in the air. The legendary hot-bloodedness of the Mexicans was nothing compared to these pale Mississippians, John thought. And he was about to wade in right up to his knees.

"I didn't sneak away in the dead of night," Emily was saying when John reached the porch. "I left in Haley Gates's wagon in broad daylight. I'm sure Dodie told you that."

"Oh, she told me, all right. And others were right quick to tell me, too. You and Sally Gates's bastard just trotting along, laughing your fool heads off all the way to Vicksburg." Elliot punched another hole in the air. "Haley Gates is going around referring to you as his friend now. His best and dearest friend! And he's telling anybody who'll listen that he'll be following you out here some day. It's scandalous, Emily. It's damned humiliating."

No wonder Price hadn't wanted to return to Russell County, John thought. He'd never truly understood his partner's reasons until now. Nor had he understood the real nature of Emily's defiance in keeping up a correspondence with Russell County's most unwelcome son. Her leaving for Texas, John understood now, was an act of bravery deserving of a medal.

"Tater'll be bringing in your luggage," he said to her.

But before Emily could reply, her brother said, "That won't be necessary. Just leave all my sister's baggage there. I'd like to buy your wagon, Bandera. And two horses." He reached into the pocket of his frock coat and withdrew a fine-grained leather wallet. "Will three hundred do?"

"They're not for sale."

"Four hundred, then? Look, man, name your price. We'd like to leave as soon as possible."

"I said they're not for sale."

"And *we're* not leaving, Elliot," Emily said. "I'm staying right here. You have no right—"

"Be still, Emily," her brother shouted. "You'll do what I tell you to do. You've caused our family all the pain and embarrassment we intend to endure."

"Then you should be glad to be rid of me, Elliot," Emily shot back.

"I won't be rid of you, you little hellion, until you're married off." He glanced around the yard, his lip curling with obvious disdain. "I don't see

Price McDaniel anywhere with a bouquet or a ring. Do you? That is why you came all this way, isn't it? To wring a proposal of marriage out of the treasonous blackguard?''

"You don't see Price because he's in Abilene, Kansas,'' she said with a sniff, then added, "On business.''

Elliot looked to John for confirmation, as if he couldn't take the word of a mere female, and this one in particular.

"He's away,'' John said, once again feeling a lie sink like a rock in his gut.

"Is he aware that my sister is here?''

John shrugged.

"Emily, I suspect your dearly beloved knows all too well that you're here, and that is precisely why he's not. I always took Price for a coward, even when he was a child. I doubt he's changed.''

"You don't know anything about him,'' Emily said. "And he's certainly not a coward. Is he, John?''

When he failed to respond, Emily pressed. "Is he, John? Cowards don't risk their lives to save others, for heaven's sake. Tell Elliot how Price saved your life when you were in the army.''

Elliot laughed. "The Union army he joined in order to get out of a Yankee prison? That army?''

"The one that won,'' John said. He angled between the sister and brother on his way to the front door. "I've got some paperwork to do. If you're planning on staying here tonight, Russell, there are plenty of spare beds in the bunkhouse. Pick out any one you want." Then he erased any note of affability from his voice when he added, "Tomorrow, I want you gone."

Emily knocked on the closed parlor door, and heard John's abrupt *venga* in reply. She wasn't sure if that meant go away or come in, so she stood there a moment, indecisive, until the door jerked open. The face scowling down on her was still taut with anger.

"My brother owes you an apology, John, but you'll never get it from him. I hope you'll accept mine, instead."

"No," he said, a small grin flicking at a corner of his hard mouth. "A lady should never offer excuses for a fool." He stepped back, gesturing her inside the parlor.

"He's used to being an important fool, I'm afraid," she said with a rueful little laugh. "Now you can probably understand perfectly why Price chose to stay here in Texas instead of coming back to Russell County."

He nodded.

Emily glanced toward his desk and the open ledger book there. "I'd like to discuss something with you, but if you're busy, it can wait."

"Not so busy," he said. "Sit. Can I have Lupe bring you a cup of coffee?"

"No, thank you." Emily settled into a chair, thinking the very last thing she needed right now, after her brother had yelled at her for the last twenty minutes, was Lupe giving her the evil eye when she was about to trespass on the young woman's terrain.

All the while that Elliot had been ranting and raving, Emily had been plotting. The scheme she'd finally settled on was far-fetched and outlandish, but it was her only hope of staying at The Crippled B. And she couldn't do it without John Bandera's help.

"Elliot wants to take me back to Mississippi," she said, trying to sound calm even though she was panicking inside. "I won't go back with him, though. I'm adamant about that, John, so I've come to ask for your help."

"Short of putting a bullet between his eyes, I don't see how I can help. He's your brother, Emily. He wants what's best for you."

"Best for me! Ha! He wants what's best for himself, which is seeing me married and out of his hair. Elliot won't be satisfied with anything less. Unfortunately, he seems to believe that my relationship with Price is just a figment of my over-wrought imagination, and no matter what I say, I can't convince him otherwise."

She paused to clasp her hands in her lap, then dropped her voice as she continued. "But I've thought of a plan, John. If only you'll listen."

He eyed her suspiciously while he angled a hip on the corner of his desk. "I'll listen."

"Elliot will leave, even somewhat happily, if he's assured that my future is secure. Since Price isn't here to demonstrate that, I thought that… well…you're here, and…perhaps you…"

He was up off the desk like a shot. "Whoa. Wait a minute, now. Just what are you asking me to do?"

Emily drew in a long breath. "More than asking. I'm begging you. If you convince my brother that you're the one who wants to marry me, he'll leave tomorrow and never look back. I won't be his responsibility anymore. He'll consider me yours. And then he'll wash his hands of me, and I'll be free."

He had walked to the window, and stood there now, staring out, not saying a word. It was almost as if he hadn't heard her.

"John? I'm begging you for your help in this. Please. Will you do this for me?" she asked.

"You want me to tell your brother that I've asked you to marry me?"

He spoke slowly, without turning around, so Emily couldn't tell if the bewilderment in his voice was visible on his face.

"It's a bald-faced lie, of course," she said, "and I know you're an honest man, not given to lying. But it would be for just a day or two. It will work. I'm sure of it."

"No, it won't. He'll never believe it."

"Coming from me, he won't," she agreed. "But if you speak to him, John, and make your intentions clear, how could he not believe it? He'll leap with joy at the prospect of my marriage. All my brother wants is for me to be somebody else's responsibility."

He turned to her now, his expression not bewildered at all, as she had imagined, but somber. Quite melancholy, actually. His amber gaze played over her face for a long time before he spoke. "He'd never allow you to marry a man like me."

"On the contrary. He'd allow me to marry anyone who didn't wear a skirt just to get me off his back. I know my brother. Believe me."

"Maybe so, but he knows you, too, and he'd never believe his sister would marry a man she didn't love."

"Then I'll pretend."

"To love me?" he asked softly.

She nodded eagerly.

He was silent again for a moment, then his serious expression gave way to a hint of a smile. "You think you could pretend well enough to convince him?"

"I know I could. I'm sure of it. Please, please say you'll help me."

"All right, then," he said. "I'll pretend to love you, too, Emily. For just a little while."

Chapter Nine

They had a late supper that evening, the three of them, in the formal dining room where Price's inlaid mahogany table and elaborately carved chairs had sat unused since his disappearance. Ordinarily John took his evening meal in the kitchen or at his desk or in the bunkhouse with his men.

John was always edgy and uncomfortable in this room. Being stared at by portraits of half a dozen pale, narrow-nosed and prim-lipped McDaniels never did much for his digestion, not to mention his mood. And that mood wasn't lifted any when Lupe served them and slapped Emily's plate on the table nearly hard enough to break it.

Elliot Russell, on the other hand, appeared to relax in these somewhat formal and familiar surroundings. ''A tad more than I expected of a ranch'' was how the man had termed it when he'd first entered the dining room, and now he was mopping up the last of Señora Fuentes's pork stew with a tortilla and great gusto while confining most of his conversation to his sister. When he did look in John's direction at the head of the table, Elliot Russell might just as well have been appraising a piece of furniture or a side of beef for all the warmth in his expression.

Across from her brother, Emily perched on the edge of her chair, picking like a sparrow at her food, glancing furtively at John, once even tapping his leg with her foot beneath the table, undoubtedly to remind him, once again, of their bargain.

As if he could forget! As if it would succeed!

How Emily could even begin to believe that her bigoted brother would hand her over to the fond, but dark embrace of a half-breed was beyond him. But futile—even cockeyed and just plain hare-brained—as John knew the scheme to be, still he'd jumped like a damned jackrabbit at the opportunity to demonstrate his love. His *pretend* love.

For at least a few sweet hours this evening he was going to be able to wear his heart prominently on his sleeve. While they were putting on their little lovestruck drama for Russell, John was already planning to close his eyes and take Emily's pretense for the real thing. He would have her for a little while. It was more, far more, than he had ever hoped for.

"John saved my life in a tornado, you know,"

Emily was saying to her brother now. "It happened shortly after I arrived."

"Is that so?" Elliot coated a last morsel of tortilla with thick russet-colored gravy and popped it into his mouth. His pale blue eyes sank closed while he chewed. "Emily, you should get that woman's recipe for this...this...whatever it is, so we can give it to Delia. It's a damn sight better than her corn bread."

"It's a tortilla," she informed him, trying hard, John noticed, to properly fold her sweet Southern drawl around the Spanish word.

"Ah," Elliot murmured. "Well, it's quite delicious. What is it? Spanish? Mexican?"

"Mexican," she told him.

"I see." He pushed back his empty plate, then leaned back and withdrew a long, thin cigar from his inside coat pocket. "You don't mind, do you, sister?"

"Not at all." She tilted her head in John's direction. "Perhaps our host would like a cigar, as well, Elliot."

He grunted, lit the cigar ceremoniously, then exhaled and squinted at John through a thick, bluish cloud of smoke. "Care for one, Bandera?"

"No. Thanks, anyway."

"Bandera," the Southerner mused aloud, his gaze moving slowly from portrait to portrait around the room. "Just what is that? Mexican, I'd bet."

"The name is," John replied, thinking it didn't take a trail blazer to figure out where the man was heading with this particular question. "But I'm not."

"Oh?"

"John is part Indian," Emily said in the same tone she might have used to inform her brother that his host had royal blood.

A pale eyebrow arched behind another cloud of smoke. "Oh, really? And what's the other part?" Elliott asked in a dry tone that seemed to assume the "other part" couldn't have been anything more civilized or acceptable than rattlesnake or skunk.

John was more than happy to fulfill his expectations. "Coyote," he said, slapping his napkin down and pushing back from the table. "It's cooled off a bit outside. Anybody for a walk?"

The sun was going down and a soft breeze was blowing up from the south, stirring the lacy mesquite leaves and riffling the hem of Emily's watered silk skirt as she walked along beside John. Her brother had declined the invitation to accompany them, much to her relief, and had chosen instead to remain on the porch with his second cigar and a small glass of tequila for want of his habitual after-dinner brandy.

"Elliot's insufferable," she said now that they were out of earshot of the house.

"You're not apologizing for him again, are you?"

The note of amusement in John's voice prompted Emily to glance up at his face. The red hues of the sunset seemed to deepen his complexion even more than usual and his eyes were a stunning, almost breathtaking shade of topaz. She thought she had never seen him more handsome than this particular moment.

And just as that thought was occurring to her, John reached for her hand and gently linked his fingers through hers.

"People in love hold hands," he said quietly. "Your brother's probably watching."

"Undoubtedly."

Emily let go of a tiny sigh, part relief that her *intended* was following through with his promise, part pleasure from the warm touch of his hand.

"Thank you, John. You were so quiet during dinner that I was worried you might have changed your mind about helping me."

"I did change my mind," he said. "Six times, at least. Maybe seven. I don't know. But now I'm right back where you wanted me."

"I'm grateful."

She glanced back over her shoulder to make certain her brother was still looking in their direction.

He was. And he was watching quite intently as far as Emily could tell. She wondered, though, if he could actually discern their gently clasped hands from such a distance. Perhaps it wasn't them that Elliott was looking at at all, but just the lovely Texas sunset that was intriguing him.

"I suppose holding hands is a subtle enough beginning," she said, tilting her head in what she hoped was a flirtatious manner. "But perhaps, John, we ought to embrace."

"All right. If that's what you want."

He stopped, drawing her to a halt, as well. Then, when his arms encircled her in a smooth, slow motion, Emily pressed her cheek against his chest and felt the hard beats of his heart reverberating throughout her own body. Like music, she thought. Such wonderful music. It matched the beating of her own heart. Their two bodies seemed so perfectly in tune.

She sighed softly, and, much to her surprise, thought she heard John do the very same thing. A little thrill raced the length of her spine. Was he, too, enjoying this ruse? she wondered. Was it pleasurable to embrace her? Even worthy of a sigh? Or was he merely attempting to thoroughly act his part?

If that was the case, his performance was first-rate, or so she assumed, having little with which to compare it. His lips were drifting over her tem-

ple now, whispering soft Spanish, while his arms
drew her even closer against him.

Close enough for her to tell that his desire for
her wasn't entirely an act.

He felt so strong, and she felt so supremely safe
within the circle of his arms. So safe. Emily closed
her eyes, allowing herself to pretend for a moment
that this was Price and that her dearest dreams
were coming true at last. It was the same thing she
had done several months ago with Alvin, forgoing
reality for the sweet embrace of her dreams. But
she hadn't really felt that safe with Alvin, had she?
In truth, she realized, she hadn't felt much of anything at all. Certainly not like this.

John's lips were so close to hers, brushing across
her cheek, that she could almost taste his softly,
warmly whispered words. They were sweet and
rich as melted chocolate.

"Corazon. Mi corazon. Te quiero."

"Your heart?" she whispered back.

"Si. My heart."

"And the other words?"

"Te quiero, Emita." His voice sounded as rough
as sandpaper and as soft as velvet, both at the same
time. Then his hands came up to gently cradle her
face, holding it still while his amber eyes burned
deeply into hers. "I love you, Emily."

Slowly, ever so slowly and sweetly, his mouth
settled over hers, all wonderful and warm and wet,

while his arms curved around her once more, drawing her body closely to his. Emily thought for a moment she might faint from lack of breath, from the sheer heat she and John seemed to be generating between them, from the exquisite pleasure of the passionate kiss.

She didn't want it to end. Ever. She didn't want to taste anything ever again except John's wonderful lips on hers. She didn't want to hear anything except his rich, melodic Spanish voice, this private and sensual music, telling her over and over again how much he loved her.

Except he didn't love her! He was simply pretending to be in love with her, living up to his end of their bargain just as she'd asked him to do.

And just as that fact had begun to crystalize somewhere in the depths of her besotted brain, Emily caught a distinct and acrid whiff of cigar smoke.

"Emily? Sister? What's going on here? What the devil is the meaning of this...this spectacle?"

John's kiss drifted away and his arms eased from around her. Emily opened her eyes, attempting to focus them on her brother's face. His livid face.

"Oh, hello, Elliot."

The huskiness of her own voice startled Emily. She hardly recognized herself. "I was just... just..."

She knew there had been a purpose to that searing, mind-shattering kiss, but just then she couldn't think of it. Or anything.

"Well? Just what?" Her brother bit down so hard on his panatela that he broke it in two. He fumed and sputtered, then he spat the remaining stub onto the ground, not far from John's boots.

Meanwhile, all Emily could do was stutter and blink.

"She just agreed to marry me," John said, stepping into the breach, not unaware of what his kiss had done to Emily's composure or her concentration. Her surprisingly ardent response hadn't left him thinking all that clearly, either, he had to admit. "I've asked Emily to be my wife."

"Your wife!" The man looked at John only long enough to communicate his cold contempt before turning back to his sister. "His wife? Why, you don't even know this…this…"

"Gentleman?" Emily offered sweetly, finally finding her tongue.

"This person," her brother spat. "It was bad enough when you sneaked away to be with that traitor, McDaniel. But agreeing to marry some…some heathen you've only just laid eyes on is…well…it's ludicrous. It's insane. It's unthinkable. I won't allow it."

John looked down at Emily, raising his eyebrows just a tad, as if to ask her if she wanted to continue the argument on her own or if she pre-

ferred that he take over now. She didn't need more
than a few seconds to make up her mind. It was
her battle, her expression said, and she proceeded
to light into her brother with a vengeance.

"You can't stop me from marrying whomever I
choose, Elliot." She took a step toward him then
and, for want of an umbrella to poke him with,
lifted her dainty, defiant chin directly into his face.
"I don't know why you'd even try to stop me or
dissuade me. After all, this is what you've wanted
ever since I turned eighteen, isn't it? To see me
married?"

"I wanted to see you to marry *well,* Emily."
His sidelong glare at John indicated that a union
with a half-breed didn't qualify on any count.

"And so I shall."

She moved closer to John now, and linked her
arm through his.

Elliot continued to scowl as he reached into his
coat pocket for a cigar to replace the one he'd bitten in two. He took a long time lighting it. Long
enough, it seemed to John, for the man to do some
mental calculations about losing a sister along with
a good bit of social stature versus gaining his free-
dom from a family responsibility he clearly didn't
relish.

After a long moment, the Southerner blew out a
thin stream of smoke, picked a fleck of tobacco

from his lower lip, and then quite calmly asked, "When?"

Emily blinked and sucked in a sharp breath. "Pardon me?"

"I asked when the two of you are planning to marry. When's the happy event?"

"Well, I... We didn't..." she stammered. "We haven't exactly..."

"Just as soon as we can get the necessary paperwork done," John told him, tightening his arm on Emily's as he felt her entire body going about as limp as five feet of wet frayed rope.

"Did you have to be that specific?"

The question fairly hissed from Emily's tightly compressed lips a little while later when they were strolling back toward the house, trailing several yards behind her brother.

Funny, John thought. He'd been asking himself the exact same question. Being specific about their wedding date had made a true believer out of Elliot Russell, that was for certain. The man might not have been overjoyed at getting a coffee-colored, black-haired, Spanish-speaking heathen for a brother-in-law, but his relief at the prospect of getting rid of his spinster of a sister—and soon!—was altogether obvious. Elliot Russell had even shaken John's hand and offered him a cigar.

John kept telling himself that he'd said what he

had about the wedding date simply because he knew it would work. And it had. Hell, it had worked like a charm!

But even though he'd gotten to be a pretty accomplished liar in the past few days, he was still no good at lying to himself. He hadn't said it for the brother's benefit at all. He'd said it because he wanted to marry Emily! That was the rock bottom truth. Just as it was the truth when he'd told her that he loved her.

It had been while he was kissing her that he had come up with a little scheme of his own, one that was just about as underhanded and addle-brained as Emily's.

"John," she said again, still whispering, but a bit more insistently now. "I don't think that was such a good idea. Telling Elliot what you did. I mean, the paperwork for a marriage probably doesn't take very long."

"A couple days, I'd guess."

"Well, there," she exclaimed with suppressed triumph. "You see?"

Yes, he did see. And what he saw so clearly now was that he had stumbled upon the perfect, once-in-a-lifetime opportunity to make her his, this woman he'd loved so long. Miss Emily Russell of Russell County, who fancied herself in love with Price McDaniel, who'd never stoop to marry anyone but a well-bred Southerner such as herself, would be his wife. John Bandera's bride.

"All I see," he answered, "is a man who appears to be pretty content to let his baby sister stay here in Texas. That was your little scheme, wasn't it? Or did I get it wrong?"

She came to a halt, jerking her arm out of his grasp, looking up at him with fierce blue fire in her eyes, trying her damnedest not to shout. "My *little scheme,* as you put it, John, didn't include a *real* marriage, for heaven's sake."

"Emily. *Mi corazon.*" He laughed softly as he reached to take her arm again. "What makes you think it would be real?"

Chapter Ten

The paperwork had only taken a single day, as it turned out, what with Elliot Russell bellowing and banging his fists on various doors and desks in Corpus Christi while shamelessly dropping the name of his illustrious cousin, Senator Russell of Mississippi. The judge was suitably impressed, and the poor man fairly flew through the marriage ceremony so Elliot could make the noon sailing of the steamship, *The Biloxi Belle.*

"Well, you're Mrs. Bandera now, sister," Elliot said, smiling down at her as they stood on the wharf.

Emily was fairly certain that the sheen of moisture in her brother's eyes had far more to do with the strong Gulf breeze than any feelings of tenderness or sentimentality on his part. He hadn't smiled at her in years, not while she remained his spinsterly burden. Come to think of it, Elliot hadn't smiled at her very much even when they were children. He had been good to her out of duty rather than affection. And now that she was John Bandera's wife, her brother's duty was done.

"Please give my love to Dodie and the children," Emily said. "Tell her I'll write often. Who knows, Elliot? Perhaps John and I will come back to Russell County for a visit in the not so distant future."

"Splendid!"

The exclamation didn't match his less-than-thrilled expression, though. Her bigoted brother was probably already wondering how he was going to explain John Bandera's deep bronze skin, high cheekbones, and long black hair. But knowing Elliot, as soon as he was back home in Russell County, he'd no doubt instigate a rumor that his sister had run off and married a Spanish grandee or perhaps a Hindu potentate.

Her groom was standing a polite distance away on the wharf, allowing them a private goodbye. Emily glanced down at her left hand now to see the faintest hint of gold through the thin lace of her glove. She had been stunned, shocked absolutely speechless, when John produced it from the pocket of his coat this morning in the judge's chambers. A wedding ring! A bright gold band! It made everything seem so...so official.

Until that moment, her scheme had seemed just

that to her. A scheme. A conspiracy, innocent enough, into which she and John had entered to allow her to remain in Texas. Then, at the sight of the thin gold ring, suddenly it seemed more sacrilege than scheme, and Emily had been sorely tempted to confess her sins and to beg her brother to take her home.

But home, she'd reminded herself, was the place where her child was destined to grow up to be known as Emily Russell's bastard. She wouldn't let that happen. She couldn't. Not if she had to marry the devil himself to prevent it.

Or perhaps she had done just that, she thought, casting a sidelong glance at John in his black frock coat, pressed trousers and shiny boots. His long hair was pulled back and tied with a black velvet ribbon, which might have made any other man look dandified, but only succeeded in making this man appear all the more masculine by disclosing the strong lines of his face and jaw. He was as handsome as the devil. If Emily knew nothing else, that she knew for certain.

"Take good care of her, Bandera," Elliot called out to him now.

A slow smile worked its way across John's lips as he sauntered toward them. "I intend to," he said, easing an arm around Emily's waist.

Foolishly, she did feel well taken care of just then. She had to remind herself once more that

John was still just playing his part, and playing it incredibly well, to boot, until the bitter end when Elliot's ship would steam away, leaving the two of them alone on the pier.

Then what? she wondered. Good Lord, what then?

The brother was gone. Good riddance. Now, as he and Emily strolled back to their hotel, John began to feel more like a man, less like an animal on display in a cage. Beside him, he heard his bride sigh softly.

"Are you happy?" he asked, gazing down at the crown of the little velvet hat that matched her dark blue dress, longing to pull out the pins and let her pale hair go spilling over her shoulders like a yellow silk shawl.

"Happy?" She repeated the word as if she couldn't quite grasp its meaning.

"Your brother is gone, and you're still here. That's what you wanted, isn't it?"

"What I wanted. Yes," she murmured, not sounding at all convinced. "But...but, John?" Her words drifted off on the warm Gulf breeze.

"Yes, Emily?"

"Now that I'm here, and now that we're... well...married, I'm wondering just what happens next?"

He had to firm his lips against a grin, keep any

hint of his current happiness out of his voice when he replied, "I don't know, *querida*. This is your little scheme. Perhaps you should tell me."

She came to a standstill then, her hand rising to steady her hat as she gazed up at him, her sweet features almost twisted in distress. "Well, that's just it, you see. I haven't the faintest idea."

John couldn't have said if it was Emily's bewilderment that struck him as funny, or if it was the sudden, nearly staggering realization that this lovely woman was his wife, but he found himself laughing all of a sudden. He hardly recognized the sound since he did it so seldom, and he had no acquaintance at all with the feeling of happiness rising up in his chest like a bird taking wing.

He was happy! *Madre de Dios!* He was the happiest man in Texas. No. On Earth!

Emily was staring at him, confused and open-mouthed and slightly goggle-eyed, as if she considered him possessed. And maybe, by God, he was. He reached out, grasped her around her waist, and lifted her high toward heaven.

"John! Have you lost your senses?"

But Emily was laughing too now, as he twirled her around and her breeze-blown skirts wrapped both of them in yard upon yard of blue.

"John, you've gone quite mad," she said in a voice more delighted than stern. "Put me down. Now. This very minute."

He didn't put her down so much as let her slowly slide the length of his body. Slowly. Sensuously. Not even her many layers of cotton and silk could keep him from knowing the delicacy of her ribs, the sweet shape of her breasts, the beat of her heart against his own.

It occurred to John just then that a bolt of lightning could strike him dead right now and he wouldn't mind one bit because, for as long as he lived, he'd never know anything sweeter, happier, or better than this.

Then, before Emily's feet quite touched the ground, while her body was snug against him and her bright blue eyes sparkled into his, he tried to speak her name, to tell her of his happiness. His voice broke in his throat, though, so he kissed her, instead.

Her lips were soft beneath his, and her mouth was generous, amazingly unafraid when he deepened the kiss as he had to do, using his tongue to taste her, his teeth to test her sweet flesh.

Wild wanting ripped through him. It was like nothing John had ever felt before. He thought his knees might buckle.

It was Emily who broke the kiss, drawing her head back, blinking, and taking in an audible gulp of air. Her face had paled considerably, in contrast with the bright spots of color on her cheeks. John couldn't read the emotions flashing across her face, but he suspected the prominent one was anger. He eased her gently down and at the same time he tensed for the slap she had every right to flay across his jaw.

When she lifted her hand, though, it was only to reposition the hat that had gone slightly out of kilter on her head, to fumble a moment with the satin piping that edged the collar of her dress, and finally to wipe away the glistening evidence of his kiss from her mouth.

It was that small gesture that brought him back to stark reality, at the same time that it nearly broke his heart.

"John!" Her voice was breathy, as if she'd just run half a mile. "I...well...I mean, we don't have to pretend anymore. My goodness. Elliot must be halfway out to sea by now, I'm sure."

He drew in a deep, cooling breath. Damned if he wanted to apologize for a kiss that meant everything to him, but he couldn't think of anything else to say. "I'm sorry, *querida*. Yes, he is gone. We don't have to pretend. I won't do that again. I swear."

Now, while Emily straightened the seams on her lacy gloves, she gave a tiny shrug. "You don't have to apologize, John," she said.

Then, cocking her head to one side, she let her gaze flutter up to his face. "It wasn't entirely your fault. I kissed you, too, you know. And it was..."

She shrugged again as if she couldn't quite decide what to say next.

"Wrong?" he suggested.

A little frown stitched her eyebrows together. "Perhaps," she said. Then her lips curved in a grin and her blue eyes twinkled while she linked her arm through his and said, "But it was very pleasant."

"Pleasant," he muttered, still feeling the not-so-pleasant effects of the kiss burning through him, unquenched and unabated. Pleasant. He wanted to laugh, to cry, to drive his fist into a wall of solid brick. What could a sheltered and overprotected lady know of the hot currents of sexual desire brought on by such a *pleasant* kiss? How could a cool, smooth-petaled gardenia, raised in a hot-house, have any inkling of such things?

She didn't. Nor would she, John vowed silently.

He sighed, then replied as lightheartedly as he could under the circumstances. "Yes, it was pleasant for me, too, *corazon*. Now, come. You must be tired after a morning of marrying and kissing. I'll take you back to your room so you can rest."

Pleasant! All the way back to the hotel Emily silently castigated herself for using such an insipid, front-parlor, Sunday-school word to describe a kiss that had been utterly indescribable.

Good Lord, it had set off fireworks in the pit of

her stomach, Roman candles in her chest, spinning pinwheels of white fire in her brain, and heat streaming all the way to her toes. It had set her aflame.

If John hadn't been holding her so tightly, she would have crumpled to the pavement and lain in a shapeless heap of soft gray ashes. Even now, several minutes since he'd put her down, her knees felt weak and buttery.

She glanced at him now as he strode beside her, wondering if the kiss had affected him similarly. But there was nothing in his expression to indicate that John felt anything other than a purposefulness about returning her to the hotel where they had spent the previous night. If the kiss meant nothing to him, Emily wondered why he'd even bothered.

And then it dawned on her. Price! John was probably feeling quite remorseful having kissed his partner's longtime lady friend. That seemed to explain his sudden silence and his nearly dour expression. Of course, it didn't explain why she, the longtime lady friend herself, hadn't spared her longtime gentleman friend so much as a single thought while her lips were pressed against his partner's.

Now she felt guilty, after the fact. Only this time, heaven help her, she couldn't use the excuse that she was pretending that her lover had been Price. It had been John Bandera kissing her. John alone.

No fantasy lover, at all. And it had been John whom she was shamelessly, even eagerly kissing back.

How, Emily wondered, could something so terribly wrong feel so wonderfully right?

Lost, even mired in her thoughts, she was surprised when John suddenly said, "Here we are," and then guided her through a wide door and into the lobby of the hotel where the three of them had spent the previous night, all in separate rooms. It was the best hotel in the city. Her brother would settle for nothing less.

Now, she and John had barely crossed the Persian carpet on their way to the staircase when they were stopped by a man in a dark blue frock coat with a drooping daisy stuck through his lapel.

"I'm afraid your rooms are no longer available, Mr. Bandera," he said.

The man was much shorter than John, which forced him to look up when he spoke. His Adam's apple poked out above his blue silk cravat.

"I've taken the liberty of packing for you. You'll find your luggage over there." He gestured toward the front desk.

Emily turned to see her hatbox and valise, along with John's blanket roll, stacked pitifully beside a potted palm. "What's the meaning of this?" she hissed at the manager. "You had no right to remove our belongings."

Rather than reply to her, the officious little man merely arched an eyebrow at John and said, "Last night you were a guest of the gentleman from Mississippi. I, ah, trust you comprehend my meaning. We don't want any problems."

Emily started to speak, but she felt John's hand tighten on her arm, silencing her. She heard him draw in a deep breath then, and when he spoke, it wasn't with indignation or anger. His voice was low and level, astonishingly cool.

"Miss Russell is very tired. At least allow her the use of a room," he said.

The manager's gaze flicked to Emily before returning to John. "Mrs. Bandera, I think you mean, don't you? Judge Avery performed a marriage ceremony this morning, I believe."

"What business is that of yours?" Emily snapped.

"Emily," John cautioned, moving closer to her, tightening his grasp on her arm.

He wanted her to be still, she could tell, but she'd be damned if she'd remain silent while this rat-faced little man tossed them bag and baggage into the street for no apparent reason. For the life of her, she couldn't understand why John was being so meek, just standing there, allowing himself to be insulted so, not to mention his wife.

"We were indeed married this morning," she

said with a little snort, wrenching off her glove in order to display the ring on her finger.

While she was waving it beneath his nose, Emily was hard-pressed not to give that ugly beak a firm and hurtful tweak.

"There. You see. We're husband and wife. How dare you imply anything the least bit improper or illicit in our behavior?"

In response, the man merely offered her a flat, cold, almost fishy stare before he raised a hand and snapped his fingers in the direction of a bellboy who was leaning against the front desk, and from the looks of him, finding the whole spectacle rather amusing.

"Andrew," the manager said, "Please put that luggage out on the sidewalk. Señor and Señora Bandera are leaving."

"No, we're—"

"Yes," John said abruptly. "We are."

Before she could say another word, John had whirled her around and was propelling her across the lobby, through the front door, and out onto the sidewalk. Barely a moment later, their belongings came sailing out the door, thumping one by one at their feet.

John dragged in a long, deep breath, knowing it wouldn't suffice to cool his rage. He'd killed men for lesser insults before the Army had taught him a measure of patience and self-control, after time had made him wiser than he'd been at seventeen.

Just breathe, he told himself, knowing the shame of the insult would pass, and along with it the anger that was burning in him. *Just breathe.*

"John?"

Emily's voice seemed distant, as if she were standing half a mile away instead of right there beside him. He hated for her to see him this way, battling for control, trying not to act the savage he'd just been accused of being. She must think him a madman. Or worse. At last, he forced himself to look down, trying to focus on her face instead of the red haze of his anger.

Her eyes were brimming with tears when they met his, and John didn't know whether his Emmy was crying from anger at being turned out of the hotel or from the stinging shame of it. In all her life, he knew, she'd never been treated that way, and the shock of it seemed to have washed all the color from her face. Only moments before that lovely face had been glowing from the aftereffects of his kiss. Now it was pale, stricken.

Now his Emmy was truly Bandera's bride—subject to the same prejudices and perils that had dogged him all of his life.

He opened his mouth to apologize, to tell her he was sorry for bringing this upon her, for ruining her life, but the words stuck in his throat. It was Emily who spoke first.

"I think we ought to return to the ranch, John," she said quietly. "I don't like it here."

Chapter Eleven

The horses seemed just as eager as their weary passengers to be returning to The Crippled B. John eased up on the reins, giving the animals their heads, allowing them to race south-southwest, across the wind, away from Corpus Christi.

Emily had spoken very little, hardly at all, during the first hour of their trip, and John had been grateful for her silence. It matched his own. Now she lay curled in the wagon bed, sound asleep. She looked like an angel, John thought each time he glanced over his shoulder.

But Texas was no place for angels. He'd have to send her back.

It was nearly dark when he pulled the wagon up in front of the house. Emily blinked sleepily when he touched her shoulder.

"Are we home?" She rubbed her eyes and yawned while struggling to sit up.

''Home,'' John told her softly, even a bit sadly to Emily's way of thinking.

It was all she could do not to reach out to touch his cheek, to whisper a reassuring *There* as she'd wanted to do so often in the hours since they'd left Corpus Christi. But his high wall of silence and his dark and brooding visage had prevented her from saying or doing anything that would remind him of their humiliating experience earlier at the hotel.

Mostly, Emily longed to tell him how proud she was of him for curbing his temper. She hadn't forgotten what he'd said to her in Santander about the cowboys who'd accosted her, and how he'd warned her not to make him kill them just because she was beautiful.

She longed to tell him how impressed she was by his restraint, how much she admired his quiet dignity, and how—if given a chance to relive this afternoon's events in the hotel—she would have driven her own fist into the manager's pale little rat face and then followed it up with solid kick to his shins.

Even more, she was aching to tell John that she couldn't imagine a stronger, gentler, finer man than he, and that she hoped, if her baby turned out to be a boy, that he would grow to manhood here at The Crippled B, away from the harsh, rude prejudices elsewhere, and that her son would turn out to be exactly like John Bandera. There was so very much Emily yearned to tell him just as soon as he was in a mood to listen.

Instead, she sighed now and merely said, "It's so good to be back."

His strong hands curved about her waist to lift her down from the wagon bed, then remained on her—warm, possessive—after her feet had met the ground. The breeze blew some of his long black hair against her cheek, and their hands touched as both of them reached for the errant strands.

John's fingers curled around hers, then he brought her hand up, softly kissing the ring he had placed there. "You must take this off now," he said.

She stared at the ring a moment. Take it off? So soon? Already it felt like a natural part of her, as if she'd worn it for years.

"It isn't real, *querida.*" He smoothed his thumb across the back of her hand. "Neither are we, you know."

"Yes, but I..."

"Take it off." His tone almost stern now. "It will only cause trouble here." He gestured toward the house at the exact moment when young Lupe stepped out onto the front porch.

"Juanito," she called eagerly.

In the light from the lantern by the door, her long, loose hair shone like a black satin shawl and her dark eyes glittered like polished ebony.

"Hola, mi Juanito," she purred sensuously.

Lupe! John's mistress! Of course he didn't want the girl to see the ring he'd put on another woman's finger as a favor, as a stage prop, out of helpfulness rather than any sort of affection.

Emily tugged at it now, trying to tear it off, but her finger was swollen, and the gold band that had slipped on so easily just this morning wouldn't budge even a quarter of an inch. The harder she pulled, the tighter it seemed to fit.

"It won't come off," she whispered frantically, watching Lupe's sleek, bare feet start down the steps on her way to the wagon. "John, it's stuck."

A rough growl came from deep in his throat, but it was stifled less than a second later when Lupe threw her arms about his neck, babbling words of obvious affection that Emily couldn't understand. Rather than gawk at the reunited lovers, Emily turned to reach back into the wagon for her hat and gloves.

She felt foolish suddenly. She felt awkward. And worse, she felt deeply wounded, as if her heart had just been bruised. It wasn't as if she hadn't known about his involvement with Lupe, she told herself. John had made no secret of that. Only…

Only nothing, she rebuked herself sharply. The fact remained that John Bandera, for all his admirable strength and impressive self-control, for all his beguiling masculine beauty, was not and never would be Price McDaniel. And if John had such a pull on her emotions and her heartstrings, Emily could only imagine how she was going to feel once Price returned to The Crippled B.

Snatching up her hat and gloves, she turned back to face the two reunited lovers. "Hello, Lupe," she said, forcing her mouth into a thin approximation of a smile.

The girl didn't smile back. Her gaze turned hard and harsh, fairly scouring Emily from head to hand to toe. Then her black eyes snapped back to Emily's left hand.

"Un anillo?" Lupe looked up at John, but he merely shrugged in reply.

"Un anillo?" She was staring at the gold band, her eyes shimmering with tears, her lips quivering. *"Juanito, cual es este?"*

"Nada," he responded through clenched teeth.

"Nada!" Lupe shrieked, tears now streaming down her cheeks while her fingers plucked frantically at John's sleeve. *"Es ella su esposa? Es la gringa su esposa?"* She stamped one bare foot and then the other. *"Di mi, Juan."*

"Silencio." He pulled his arm away, then shifted to his right, putting himself between Emily and the enraged young Mexican girl.

Their conversation continued, hot, hotter, blazing back and forth, sizzling in a heated Spanish, not a word of which Emily could even begin to understand. She did, however, comprehend that the confrontation was over, at least temporarily, when she heard Lupe spit and then lash the flat of her hand across John's cheek before she went running back to the house.

John stood there a moment, his back to Emily, heat radiating from every inch of him as he ripped his fingers through his hair and uttered a few more curses in the direction of the fleeing Lupe.

Emily grimaced as she tried once more to extract her swollen finger from the ring. She muttered a few choice curses of her own.

"If I just had some soapy water, I think I could slip this off. Or some butter. Or a spoonful of lard. That might do the trick."

"Don't worry about the blasted ring," he told her gruffly. "It's too late now." As he spoke, he was reaching around her for her hatbox and valise.

Still, Emily continued to twist the tight gold band. "I'm sure, once Lupe calms down, you'll be able to explain the situation. She'll forgive you once she understands. She'll have to."

"You think so, do you?" He was staring down at her now, a wistful little smile stitched across his lips. "Well, that may be, Emily, but right now I'm more worried about her forgiving you."

"Me?"

"*Si, corazon.* If you spoke Spanish, you would know that little Lupe just said she was going to the kitchen to get a knife, and that after she stuck the blade into my black heart, she was going to plunge it into yours.''

Emily blinked. ''She can't mean that.''

''Oh, she means it, all right. Now, come. I want you inside where you're safe.''

Inside the house, John climbed the stairs behind Emily, staying as close as he could possibly get in spite of her trailing skirts. He cursed himself for not having the foresight to get rid of that wedding ring long before they arrived. He'd had a feeling that his housekeeper's possessive daughter would explode if she suspected her rival had defeated her.

He'd only expected an explosion of angry tears, though. The knife he hadn't anticipated. He should have. He suspected the girl was hot-tempered and jealous enough to try to use it.

Mujeres! Women! How was it that such beautiful, delicate creatures could wreak such havoc in a man's life?

He thought if he had it all to do over, he never would have written that letter to Mississippi and, when Señora Fuentes had arrived with a hot-blooded daughter in tow, he would have sent both of them straight back to Mexico and done all of the housework himself.

Behind him, he could hear Lupe screaming in the kitchen. Every curse was punctuated by a slamming drawer or the shattering of a dish. *Dios.* He'd be lucky to have a saucer to eat off once the black-eyed beauty's tantrum was over.

"John! Please don't push me," Emily hissed at him now over her shoulder. "I can't climb these stairs any faster. I'm tripping on my skirts as it is."

He muttered an apology, eased the pressure from his hand on her back, thinking he ought to just pick her up and carry her the rest of the way. He was about to do just that when Lupe screamed again, this time from the bottom of the staircase. When he looked over his shoulder, the girl was already partway up the stairs, and John had only a second to react to the long and lethal knife clenched in her upraised hand.

He pushed Emily forward, then pivoted, lifting his forearm to deflect the blade while reaching out a hand to grab the girl by the throat, the hair, any-where he could get a firm hold on her. At the same instant that he felt the knife slice through his sleeve, his fingers tangled in Lupe's long hair and he jerked her sharply to the right, pulling her off balance.

Lupe went down hard against the banister, shrieking in pain now instead of jealous rage. John reached for the knife still clenched in her hand, only dimly aware that Emily's skirts were hinder-

ing his movement, that his bootheels were caught
up in swirls of ruffled silk petticoats.

Then suddenly it was Emily who was crying out,
clutching at his sleeve, as she tumbled past him.
He dropped the knife to reach for her with both
hands, but it was too late.

The silk of her skirt ripped out of his hands and
his Emily fell, head over heels, stair after stair after
stair, down—a long, sickening, bone-shattering
distance.

Emily couldn't catch her breath. She was lying
at the bottom of the staircase, and even though her
eyes were open wide, everything appeared blurred
and oddly tinted, like daguerreotypes in which the
subjects hadn't been able to hold still.

She had fallen down the stairs. That much she
knew. The terrible tumble seemed to have taken an
eternity. By all rights she ought to have broken her
neck along with countless other bones, but nothing
felt broken. She wasn't in any pain at all. She simply couldn't think straight.

John's face hovered over her and his lips were
moving, but his voice seemed to come from far
away when he asked her if she was all right.

Yes. She wasn't sure if she had actually spoken
the answer or merely thought it. Then John was
gathering her in his arms, lifting her up against
him, turning. She felt dizzy for a moment, and then

she was adrift in a warm, peaceful darkness that she didn't want to leave for a very long time.

Soon there was the comfort of a mattress, the touch of cool sheets and a downy pillow beneath her head. She wanted to sleep, listening to the lullaby sounds of the soft, lilting Spanish going back and forth between Mrs. Fuentes and John.

"Emily? Can you hear me?"

John's warm, callused hand was smoothing back her hair from her forehead. His voice was so soft, so gentle. She could feel his warm breath on her cheek.

"Listen to me, Emily. I don't think you broke any bones, but there's blood. Señora Fuentes wants me to ask if this is your time of the month."

Month? She tried to recall exactly what month it was. July? No. She'd been in Mississippi in July. It was August now. She was certain.

"Querida," John said more insistently. "You are bleeding. Listen to me. Open your eyes."

His hands curved around her shoulders now and he shook her enough to make her want to push him away. "We have to know if this is normal, Emily, or if you are badly injured."

What? What was he asking? He was speaking in English but somehow she wasn't comprehending. Was she bleeding? She remembered the girl with the knife now. She remembered Lupe screaming and her black eyes flashing as the girl ran up the stairs with the knife in her hand. Was that it? Emily wondered. Had she been stabbed?

She tried to elbow up, but John wouldn't let her. His hands were on her shoulders like two warm, oppressive weights. They grasped her more tightly now.

"Emily, you have to tell me. This is important. Is it your time of the month?"

"No, I..."

She opened her eyes. All of a sudden, everything unscrambled and the pieces of her brain that had felt like scattered puzzle parts seemed to come together.

Her baby!

She'd had a terrible fall. There was blood. Oh, dear God. John's face was close to hers, his amber gaze intent, as if he were trying to read her mind.

Behind him Mrs. Fuentes said something that caused him to snap at her over his shoulder, *"No. Es imposible."*

"What?" Emily asked. "What's impossible? What's wrong?"

He shook his head. "Señora Fuentes says perhaps you are miscarrying. She wants me to ask if you are going to have a baby, but I told her that's crazy. It's not possible."

"Oh, God." The tears came so fast then that Emily couldn't even blink them away. Her throat closed painfully, preventing her from speaking even if she knew what to say.

John's face—that handsome, worried face—disappeared in a hot salty blur. "It's not possible," he said again, less certainly now. "Emily? Is it?"

"Please," she managed to whisper. "Please, John. You mustn't tell Price. I need to tell him in my own time, in my own way. Promise me."

He didn't promise. He didn't say anything at all except to exhale a low and gutteral curse. When she reached for his sleeve, he pulled away. Then the mattress shifted abruptly and a second later, the bedroom door slammed closed.

John slammed the front door behind him, kicked over a slat-back chair on the porch, then stalked toward the corral. Five minutes later he had bridled the mare, Corazon, and was riding her bareback, running her flat out, away from the house, away from the woman who lay upstairs there, away from everything.

If he had stayed a second longer, he might have done her and her baby harm. God forgive him, but there had been that one hot, blinding instant when his fingers could have circled her smooth white neck and choked the life out of her, when his hands could have shaken her until every one of her delicate white bones snapped like brittle twigs.

Then, only a moment after wanting to strangle

Emily, his fury changed directions and he wanted to murder the man who had touched his Emmy, kissed her, loved her, left his seed so deep inside her.

An instant after that, he was furious with himself for being taken in by her wide-eyed innocence and her calculated maidenly airs, for being duped as thoroughly as any hayseed ever had, and for loving her still in spite of her deceit.

Now, riding nowhere, only away, trying not to think, trying not to feel, John wanted to reach up and rip the moon right out of the sky. He wanted to punch a hole in heaven, to sink his fist in the face of God, to fall to his knees, weeping, and never get up.

He pushed the mare harder, faster, farther away from the house. He dug his heels into her flanks and his toes into her ribs. He pushed her brutally, until her hot spittle flew back in his face to mix with the tears that tracked down his cheeks.

He rode her without mercy until the mare's back grew so lathered and slippery that John could hardly keep his seat, until Corazon finally screamed pitifully and stumbled hard, and pitched him headlong, dazed and half-crazy, into the sharp thorns of a mesquite.

Chapter Twelve

Early the next day John washed up in the deserted bunkhouse, grateful that all his men were still away so he wasn't obliged to explain his red-rimmed eyes and the numerous cuts on his face and hands.

He looked like he'd been on the losing side of a catfight, he thought. No, he looked like a crazy man who'd spent the better part of the night in the fierce embrace of a mesquite bush while he howled pitifully at a deaf heaven and shook his fists at the sightless moon.

Que idiota. What a fool.

But, foolish or not, he'd come to a few decisions this morning, once his head had cleared sufficiently enough to think. Now, while he stared in the cracked bunkhouse mirror and gingerly shaved off two days' worth of stubble, John tried to convince himself that those decisions were the right ones.

First, Señora Fuentes and her daughter would

have to leave. The sooner the better. He would pay the woman a full month's wages in severance pay, write her a glowing letter of recommendation that overlooked the fact that she had a lusty, knife-wielding daughter, and then he'd have Tater Latham take them wherever the *señora* wanted to go. Corpus Christi. Matamoros. Nuevo Leon. It didn't matter where they went as long as their destination was far enough away to keep Lupe from returning. He hated to deprive Emily of his housekeeper's care and womanly expertise, especially now, but there was no way around it. He would never be able to trust hotheaded Lupe in the same house with his wife and child.

John had said those words out loud not so long ago to the footsore mare as he walked her back to the corral. *My wife and my child.* Now he held the razor still against his cheek and whispered the words once more. My wife and my child.

There would be no sending Emily back to Mississippi now. He could only imagine how the gentlefolk of Russell County treated their tarnished kin. The good people of Texas weren't all that forgiving, either, when it came to bastards. But, since he and Emily were already married, that wasn't going to be a problem. There would be no bastards at The Crippled B.

There would be no pretense of a marriage, either. There would be no divorce. Emily was and would forever be Señora Bandera. She was his wife, and her child would be his child.

He searched his reflection in the mirror above the soapy washbowl, unable to suppress the smallest flicker of a grin.

This was what he'd always longed for, wasn't it? He couldn't have planned it better, he thought. His dream truly had come true. A little crooked perhaps. A little shy of innocence. But he could live with that easily enough. His Emmy's past didn't matter anymore. There was only the future to consider.

And for the very first time in his life, John felt like a man with a future.

When Emily heard the commotion downstairs, she drew in a deep breath and sat up a little straighter against the huge mountain of pillows against the headboard behind her. Even if she couldn't understand the words that flew furiously back and forth, she understood only too well the emotions behind them. It was a bit like listening to an opera.

John played the part of the outraged baritone, she decided. Mrs. Fuentes was the sorrowful soprano. And then there was Lupe, all hot indignation and foot stamping, punctuated by an occasional shriek.

The melodrama seemed to go on for hours,

which suited her just fine because when John was finished with his housekeeper and her daughter, Emily was fairly certain she would be the next one to feel the sting of the man's bad temper.

She shifted her shoulders against the pillows, then sighed as she smoothed the counterpane and pressed it across her slightly rounded stomach.

"It's all right," she whispered to the baby growing there. "I won't let him send us away. I'll do anything, whatever I have to do, to make him let us stay."

When she heard the unmistakable sound of John's footsteps on the stairs, Emily's first instinct was to jump out of bed and race in the opposite direction. Mrs. Fuentes had made it fairly clear, though, in a combination of words and gestures, that for the sake of her child she was to stay in bed, at least until the bleeding stopped. So Emily didn't move. She merely held her breath as the footsteps neared her closed door.

John rapped softly. "Emily, may I come in?"

She let out her breath just a bit. He didn't sound unreasonably angry. In fact, his voice was gentle. If he was going to throw her out, at least he intended to do it in a civilized fashion.

"Yes, of course," she called out. "Come in."

He didn't stomp into the room as she might have expected, but rather walked softly and smoothly, across the small Persian rug and the polished wood floor, his eyes on hers all the while. Somehow he reminded her of a tomcat, gracefully wary as it came near something or someone unknown. His expression was somber, almost grim, as he approached.

The edge of the bed halted his progress. "May I sit?" he asked.

"Certainly."

She shifted to her left a little, not only to give him room, but to put a bit more distance between them. But when the mattress canted beneath his solid weight, she found herself sliding back, her leg firmly pressed against his immoveable hip.

"How are you feeling this morning?" he asked. "Better?"

She nodded. Well, was the man going to turn her out or not? If so, it seemed the gentlest, even the most hesitant of evictions.

"Good," he murmured. "That's good."

Then he fell strangely silent while his amber eyes remained almost studiously upon her, searching her face as if something were written there, faint letters he found difficult to read.

It was only then that she noticed that John's lovely eyes were rimmed in red and that his handsome face was etched with scratches, and before she even realized it, Emily had lifted her hand and had pressed her palm to his warm, afflicted cheek.

"Lupe?" she inquired softly.

A mournful little laugh broke from his throat and he shook his head. "No, not Lupe. I had a losing argument with a mesquite bush last night. You don't have to worry about Lupe anymore, *querida.* I'm sending her and her mother away. Far away."

"Oh. I see."

Emily's hand dropped to her lap, and she braced herself for his next pronouncement. After all, if he could send his own young mistress packing, how difficult would it be to give his partner's lady friend the boot?

"The *señora* says you must stay here, in bed, at least a week after the bleeding stops," he said, eyeing her almost sternly now. "Did she make that clear to you? Were you able to understand?"

Emily nodded. "I didn't know exactly how long, but I did understand I wasn't supposed to get up. A whole week?" Emily tried to disguise the sudden optimism in her voice. "You're sure that's what she said? A week?"

"I'm sure."

She could feel the tension fairly seeping out of her shoulders and neck while the knot of worry began to loosen in her chest. Because of her perilous condition, John had just granted her a stay of execution for a week.

Why, anything could happen in a week!

Wasn't she herself the living proof of that, having traveled from Mississippi, survived a tornado, gotten herself married, and then tossed down a flight of stairs in practically the same amount of time? Emily firmed her lips against even the hint of a hopeful smile.

John kept looking at her as if there were more he wanted to say, but didn't quite know how. Then his gaze flickered in the general direction of her stomach before returning to her face. "The little one," he said softly. "When is it due?"

"December, I believe."

"December," he echoed. "A Christmas baby. That's a sign of good luck."

"Is it?" Emily was feeling anything but lucky at the moment, wondering where she'd be come Christmas.

"And the father?" John's voice was just a rough whisper. "Is he…?"

"Dead."

"I see."

He lapsed into another mysterious silence then, this time staring down at the floor. For the life of her, Emily couldn't figure out what John was thinking or feeling. His face was a dark mask. His eyes betrayed nothing. Neither sympathy nor disgust nor curiosity.

She wondered if he was waiting for her to offer some sort of explanation of how she came to be this way, perhaps some sad details of star-crossed lovers that might make her condition more acceptable in his sight.

It occurred to her then that she might tell him she'd been raped, thus excusing herself of any responsibility for her pregnancy whatsoever. But as soon as the notion played through her mind, Emily dismissed it.

It was one thing to deceive her brother with a contrived marriage. Deceiving John Bandera, now that he knew about her baby, was unthinkable. She respected his intelligence too much, and she knew instinctively that he would find more dishonor in dishonesty than in bearing an illegitimate child.

"Believe it or not," she said, "It was just that one time. And we didn't…"

"Ssh." John silenced her with a light finger to her lips. "It's not for me to know."

She smiled just the wisp of a smile, not knowing whether it was from the tender touch of his finger or from relief in not having to dredge up her sordid past.

At the same time, she couldn't help but wonder if Price's reaction would be half so chivalrous as John's. Probably not. John, after all, had no claim on her. Well, other than a very legal document testifying to a very false marriage.

"We'll talk about this later," he said, easing off the bed. "You should sleep now. I'll be close by if you need anything. Just call me."

She settled back into the pillows. "You've been good to me, John. I'm grateful. I hope you know that."

"*Si.* I know. Now sleep."

As the door latch clicked behind him, Emily closed her eyes. John Bandera was a good man, despite a certain propensity toward violence. He was an honest, even a caring man.

Sometimes there were moments—little flashes of intuition, brief glimpses which disappeared as quickly as they came—that made her think she knew him far better than she actually did. Sometimes he looked at her as if he felt the same, as if he truly recognized her as more than Price's friend. If she gave any credence to the claims of fortune-tellers and palm readers, she might be tempted to believe that she and John had known each other in some past life.

Still, it was this life that concerned her. And now she had to figure out some way to stretch a one week's stay of execution into a lifetime.

Lupe was waiting for him at the bottom of the stairs. Her long hair was brushed to a black as glossy as a raven's wing. The young woman stood with her arms crossed, flaunting her tawny breasts above the soft and gaping neckline of her thin white *camisa*. One bare foot was tapping.

John descended the stairs, making a mental shift

from his Emmy, the fragile gardenia, to the thorny
rose who awaited him. It occurred to him quite
unexpectedly that, if things had been different, his
housekeeper's daughter could easily have been his
wife right now. If it hadn't been for his feelings
for Emily, he doubted he would have had the will,
let alone the desire, to steel himself so long against
Lupe's beauty and her brazen charms.

Caramba. He had an appetite for women, it was
true, and he considered himself a starving man, but
it was the fallen angel upstairs who tempted him.
Not the devilish beauty below.

He took the stairs slowly, wondering how the
devil he was going to keep fending Lupe off, how
he could keep her away from Emily without re-
sorting to a rope or a chain, when Tater Latham
suddenly walked in the front door.

''I'm back, boss,'' he said.

''Good,'' John replied. ''And just in time. I have
another job for you.''

He had reached the bottom of the stairs now,
and without saying another word, he bent his
knees, grabbed Lupe around her slender hips, then
stood with a hundred pounds of squealing, kicking,
flailing female draped over his shoulder.

''I want you to drive Señora Fuentes and her
daughter wherever they want to go.''

Tater, still covered with dust from his ride in

from the line shack, scraped off his hat and scratched his head. "What? Today?"

"Now."

The word came out roughly because Lupe's knee had just slammed into John's chest and her fists were pounding his shoulder blade and ribs. "The señora's already packing their belongings," he said, heading for the front door.

Tater promptly sidestepped to avoid the flying fists and feet, but managed to get clipped on the ear anyway as John strode past him and through the doorway, then out to Tater's still-hitched wagon where he deposited Lupe in back with a water barrel, a keg of nails, and assorted lengths of rope and lumber.

"See that she stays there, Tater," he ordered, "while I help the señora finish up her packing."

"Right, boss."

As John turned to go back to the house, he heard, just beneath Lupe's wild shrieks and curses, the distinct sound of Tater's Navy Colt clearing leather, its hammer cocking, while the cowhand drawled almost sleepily, "Just you sit tight there, Miss Lupe, you little hellcat."

Any other time, that lazy, lethal warning would have brought a smile to John's lips. But not right now. He'd smile, he decided, after the little hellcat was gone.

* * *

But after Lupe and her mother had been gone for almost two days, John wasn't smiling at all.

He had taken over the housekeeper's duties with enthusiasm at first, selecting the plumpest chicken in the yard to make a hearty chicken soup for Emily. Once the chicken was plucked, he'd chosen onions and carrots from the vegetable garden and a few perfectly shaped, unspotted potatoes from the kitchen larder.

After the kettle had been on the stove an hour, he tasted the hot broth, decided it needed salt, then promptly dropped not only the measuring spoon but the entire box of salt into the brew.

Things went downhill from there.

He embarrassed Emily when he was clumsy retrieving the chamber pot from beneath her bed. Then, after making her face flame again when he gathered up her bloodstained petticoats and underclothes, he discovered he couldn't remove the stains from the garments no matter how long he boiled them.

It didn't help that two of his returning cowhands rode in while he was pinning them to the line, joking that they must have the wrong place, asking for directions to The Crippled B, and once even calling him *Juanita*.

Ay de mi!

The second night, after scorching Emily's petticoats instead of ironing them, he climbed the staircase feeling as if he'd been beaten by an irate mob wielding wet mops and broomsticks.

Emily called softly to him when he reached the top of the stairs. The lamp beside her bed was still burning when he peeked into her room.

"Are you all right?" he asked.

"I'm fine. I just can't sleep. I was wondering if you could do me a favor, John."

"Anything."

She pointed toward the bureau on the far wall. "There's a bundle of letters in the middle drawer. If it wouldn't be too much trouble…"

"No. No trouble at all." He crossed the room, pulled open the drawer, only to be greeted by his own handwriting on a well-worn envelope. The stack was tied with a delicate blue ribbon.

"From Price?" he asked, putting it into her outstretched hand.

"Yes." She sighed wistfully as her fine, pale fingers played over the paper, as John watched the lamplight weave bright golden threads through her unbound hair. "Sometimes…"

Tell her, John said to himself. *Tell her now.*

"Sometimes I just miss him so," she went on. "It's silly, I suppose. They're only letters, and yet they make me feel I'm with him somehow."

Tell her, you cobarde. You gutless coward.

"You've been so good to me, John," she said, but even as she spoke, she seemed to be regarding him as an intruder upon her privacy, a most unwelcome stranger. The patience on her face was strained, and the light in her eyes, that anticipatory gleam, wasn't for him at all, but rather for a fine Mississippi gentleman who didn't exist anywhere but in her dreams.

How could he tell her the truth, and dash those sweet hopes and dreams and desires? How could he hurt her that way, this delicate gardenia?

Perhaps even worse, how could he confess, then stand by as he watched all of his own dreams die in her scornful face? It was better, for now, to keep their separate dreams alive. Let her be happy in her love for a nonexistent Price, rather than miserable loving no one.

"I'll leave you to your reading," he said. "I'll be downstairs at my desk if you need me. I may just do some reading myself."

He thought of the letters from Mississippi locked away in the safe downstairs, the letters he hadn't needed to read anymore since the day their author had arrived. Reading them again tonight would be unbearable, knowing that at the same time Emily read his letters upstairs. To be so close and yet so lonely. *Ayi.* It made him want to cry.

John swallowed the hard lump in his throat. "Sleep well, Emily."

"Thank you, John. I hope you do the same. Good night."

Then she was already lost in a letter—his letter—already smiling wistfully, lovingly, as he left the room.

Chapter Thirteen

When Emily's week was finally up, she wasn't even tempted to prolong her confinement in order to avoid the risk of being sent away. Bed rest, in her opinion, left a lot to be desired.

She was half-crazy from staying in bed with nothing to do but memorize the wallpaper or stare through the window at the changing colors of the sky. Even Price's letters no longer sufficed to alleviate her boredom, and she'd begun to feel more than a little guilty having John wait on her day in and day out.

By now, most of the hired hands had returned to The Crippled B, but John wouldn't allow anyone to care for her but himself. And day by day, while Emily had improved, her nurse-cook-chamber maid had begun to look as if he could have benefited from a weeklong stay in bed himself. There were dark circles beneath his eyes and

the set of his mouth seemed frozen in a downward
slant, permanently grim.

How she missed those wonderful grins that
every so often used to blaze across his handsome
face!

As she dressed on the morning of the eighth day,
Emily couldn't help but smile at the scorch marks
on her petticoats. Capable man that he was, John
Bandera was no housekeeper. With Mrs. Fuentes
and her daughter gone, The Crippled B was in sore
need of a woman to cook and iron and mend and
clean. Even though Emily had never done a single
household chore in her life, she was ready to offer
her services now. When John said go, she was fully
prepared to give him a hundred reasons why she
should stay.

Chief among her reasons, of course, was Price,
who still hadn't returned. Each time she inquired
about him, John shrugged and quickly changed the
subject. And much as she longed for Price's company, Emily had to admit that she was relieved not
to have to face him just yet or to explain her condition.

That condition seemed quite stable now. She
hadn't noticed even a speck of blood since the day
after her fall down the stairs, and the flutterings
inside her burgeoning belly felt healthy and strong.
Her child was secure. She was sure of that. Now
all she had to do was secure it a place in this world.

She was a little light-headed going down the stairs, so she paused, holding tight to the banister, forcing herself to breathe deeply and evenly, telling herself that this was quite normal under the circumstances. After being horizontal for a week, it wasn't all that surprising that her body resisted being upright.

By the time she reached the kitchen, the dizziness had passed, except for the instant of breathlessness when Emily saw John coming through the back door with a basket of eggs in one hand and a bouquet of wildflowers in the other. His face immediately hardened in a scowl.

"You shouldn't be up," he said, depositing the basket and the flowers on a table.

"I shouldn't be a lazy stay-a-bed now that I'm perfectly well," she said, dismissing his objection with the wave of her hand while she tried to smile and sound quite casual. "What lovely flowers! Shall I arrange them in a vase?"

John caught her hand as she reached for the bouquet.

"Are you sure you're well enough?" he asked. "Are you certain the child is all right?"

"I've done just as Mrs. Fuentes told me, John. I've been in bed for a full week and I'm quite back to normal," Emily insisted. "I think it's high time I started to earn my keep around here, don't you?"

She gazed hopefully around the kitchen, acting

as if it were her natural habitat. "Where would you like me to begin?"

"Right here."

He pulled out a chair, firmly but gently guided her into it, then wrenched another chair from beneath the table and proceeded to straddle it as if it were a small but obstreperous pony.

"I've reached one or two decisions this past week," he said. "Decisions about you and this child."

"Oh?"

Suddenly all of Emily's bright hopes seemed to sputter out, and a feeling of dread lodged in her chest as she sat there waiting for John's proclamation, waiting for him to pass sentence on her. From the determined look on his face, no argument would sway him. Nothing she could say was going to change his mind or her fate.

"I'm taking you to Santander, Emily," he said. "Just as soon as you feel up to traveling."

"I see."

No, she didn't see at all. She couldn't see for the hot tears that were suddenly blinding her. Biting her lip to keep from crying, she asked, "Do I have any choice in the matter?"

Her question seemed to take John completely by surprise, judging from the way he blinked and shifted in the chair. "I thought you enjoyed the company of Hy Slocum's wife," he said.

"Sarah? Yes, I did enjoy her company, but what does that have to do with anything, John?"

His gaze, usually so forthright and honest, cut away from Emily now, while he appeared to be searching for just the right words to banish her. Always the gentleman, she thought bleakly. Damn him.

"You need to be," he began almost sheepishly, "close to a woman who's had some experience with childbirth. Now that Señora Fuentes is gone, there's no one here who can do you or your baby any good if something goes wrong. Besides Sarah Slocum's help, there's a doctor who visits Santander several times a year, too."

"So you're sending me away for my own good?" As desolate as she felt, it was difficult to keep the sarcasm out of her voice.

"Yes," he answered. "I guess you could put it that way. It's for your good as well as the child's. I wouldn't want anything to happen to either one of you as long as I could prevent it."

How, she wondered, could anyone so kind be so cruel?

She let out a long sigh. "Oh, John."

And now he reached out to smooth his hand across her cheek. "It's because I care about you, *querida,* as well as this baby of yours."

Emily leaned away from the soothing warmth of his fingertips. What good was it, anyway, that he cared for her or that she cared for him when he was so determined to banish her from The Crippled B?

Without looking at him, she got up and walked toward the door. "I'll pack my belongings now. I'll be ready whenever you say."

"Emmy?"

The pet name brought her up short, and she turned to face him once more. Had he changed his mind? "Yes?"

"It isn't so far away. Santander."

"Isn't it, John? Right now it seems like more than a million miles."

John sat there, watching her disappear through the doorway, feeling his tongue tied tighter than a calf rope around a saddle horn. The flowers he'd meant to give her lay forlornly on the table, wilting just as Emily's smile had wilted when he'd told her his plan.

No, he corrected himself. He'd only told her part of his plan. He hadn't mentioned the part about loving her and her baby, about wanting to be husband and father and protector of them both. For a man who could be so eloquent on the page, he'd turned out to be no better than an illiterate boy when it came to expressing his love.

He could hear Emily upstairs, opening and closing drawers as she collected her belongings. It occurred to him then that she had probably misunderstood his intention, that she assumed he meant to leave her with the Slocums in Santander indefinitely.

Ay, Juanito. Say what you mean, you bloodless coward. Even if she doesn't love you, the woman will be grateful for her baby's legitimacy. Then, maybe someday that gratitude could turn to love.

He snatched up the bouquet, more determined than ever to face Emily and to make his feelings known. He took the stairs two at a time, propelled by his need to speak, but when he stood in her doorway, his words stuck in his throat, a logjam of emotion, while he watched her pressing one of his letters to her breast. Even from that distance, he could see that her cheeks were wet with tears.

''Emmy, please don't cry,'' he said, stepping over the threshold.

The letter fell from her hand and fluttered to the floor like some dead thing. The expression on her face was that of someone in deep mourning. Her blue eyes had gone as gray as wet winter skies, and when she finally spoke her voice was grief-stricken and barely audible.

''He's dead, isn't he, John? Otherwise, why wouldn't Price have sent some word by now?''

''I don't know.''

It was the truth, but the words left a bitter taste in his mouth nevertheless. John cursed the day seven years ago that Price McDaniel not only saved his life, but altered its course forever.

"Then he's done this before?" she asked, blinking back her tears. "Simply disappeared? Without so much as a letter or a fond wave farewell?"

John shrugged. "Once or twice. As partners go, Price isn't the most reliable."

She bent to pick up the fallen letter, then stared at it as if it were written in a foreign language. "In all these years, I never had the slightest inkling of that waywardness. The man I came to know in our correspondence was solid, trustworthy, the very soul of responsibility."

Taking the paper from her hand, John looked at his own penmanship. It was like looking at his own face in a mirror with all its familiar lines and twists and grooves. "The written word can be deceiving sometimes, I guess."

"But I was counting so on that responsible nature of his. I was hoping…" Her hand fluttered over her abdomen before dropping to her side. "I admit I was hoping that Price would agree to be a father to this child of mine. Or, if nothing else, at least to give the poor thing a legitimate name."

"Seems to me," John said as casually as he could while his heart was in his throat, "that your baby's already got a name, Mrs. Bandera."

"But that's…" Her startled gaze flew up to

meet his. "I don't understand you at all. How can you say that when you're sending me away?"

"Only for a little while so you can have the companionship of a woman. I told you that. Didn't I say I wanted what was best for you?"

"I know what you said, John, but I thought you were just trying to be kind, to soften the blow, so to speak." Her wide eyes narrowed now with distrust even as they glittered with hope. "Are you telling me that I'm welcome to come back here, to remain here indefinitely with the child?"

He nodded, unable to frame any of the pretty speeches he'd practiced in his head, still too much the tongue-tied coward, too afraid this beautiful woman he loved so much would find a reason to decline his offer. While he stood there, speechless, Emily drifted away from him toward the window where she gazed out silently. Unable to see her face, John could only imagine the expression of uncertainty there, perhaps even disappointment.

"We could learn to be a family," he said. "We've already done the paperwork." He moved to stand behind her, and reached down for her left hand. "The ring is here on your finger."

Emily laughed softly, allowing her hand to remain in his. "That's because I still can't get the confounded thing off."

"Then perhaps this was meant to be." He pressed his lips to her fingertips. "Perhaps it is our fate, you and I and the little one. What do you think of that, *mi corazon?*"

Emily didn't answer immediately, but she seemed to relax a bit, tilting her head back so it rested against John's chest. Finally she let out a deep sigh and said, "I don't know what to think, John, only that I do believe I'll miss you during my stay in Santander. Will you visit me there?"

"Of course." He lowered his head, letting his lips play softly against her hair, resisting the urge to turn her and kiss her.

"Or, if visiting isn't possible," she said, "perhaps you could write me a letter now and then."

"I'm not so good at letters, Emily," he lied. "I'll come to you. As often as you like."

The following day, still intent on taking her to Santander, John made a bed for Emily in the back of the wagon, piling it high with a mattress and quilts and pillows, so that she nearly sat upright while she watched the landscape of The Crippled B fall away behind them. It struck her as oddly symbolic that she had a clear picture of where she had been while the road up ahead remained a mystery.

John had offered to be the father of her child. That fact still amazed her. Whether it was out of generosity or gallantry, Emily wasn't sure. She'd hardly been able to speak when he told her both she and the baby were welcome back at the ranch.

She had wanted to turn and melt into his arms with gratitude. John Bandera had turned out to be as solid and responsible as she had ever dreamed that Price could be. It wasn't a fate Emily would ever have foreseen.

It was, however, a fate that became a bit more intriguing with every passing moment. And Emily had to admit that she'd been thinking about John a good deal, and that those thoughts were often not simply about his generous nature or his fine character, but rather about the man himself with his strong features and his hard-muscled physique.

Just this morning, when he had picked her up in his arms to place her in the wagon bed, a kind of heat had flowed through her from her toes all the way to the top of her head. And once he'd settled her in the pile of quilts and pillows, she'd been ever so reluctant to withdraw her arms from around his neck. She'd even thought how wonderful it would be if he had chosen to kiss her at that moment. Her lips had even pursed in anticipation.

He hadn't kissed her, though, but rather extracted himself from her arms and then turned his full attention to the horses and their gear. The same sense of disappointment that had coursed through her earlier came back now, making her feel foolish.

John Bandera, after all, had married her out of generosity, not out of love. And he was willing to remain married to her out of a gallant sense of responsibility that had nothing to do with any feelings he might have for her.

To assume anything else was a silly, schoolgirlish fantasy, she decided, and she ought to consider herself lucky to have the man's name rather than wasting her time wanting his heart, as well.

As for her own heart, hadn't that belonged to Price for years? She supposed it always would, whether or not he returned. Just then, the wagon rattled over and down a small rise, and Emily caught her last glimpse of the house at The Crippled B. She sighed softly and closed her eyes, rocking with the rhythm of the wagon, dreaming of the day she'd finally be returning, a baby in her arms.

Emily awoke with John's warm hands on her shoulders and his cool shadow across her face. She blinked away the foggy remnants of her sleep and asked, "Are we here, John? So soon?"

"You were asleep most of the way," he said. "And it isn't soon. It's nearly sunset."

When she started to struggle up, awkward with sleepiness and the extra pounds she was carrying, John slipped his arms around her, pulling her easily to a sitting position from which she could see the fierce orange circle of the setting sun just beyond his shoulder. To her left stood the worn and weathered clapboards of Hy Slocum's saloon. She remembered it well, and suddenly Emily realized just how sorely she had missed female companionship, so she peered through the front entrance, eager to see Sarah Slocum's pretty, cheerful face.

"You were right about this visit, John. It's going to be wonderful spending time with Sarah."

"I expect she'll feel the same way," he answered. "Come on. Let's get you down, then you can take up with Sarah while I bring in your bags."

He lifted her down from the wagon, but instead of letting her go, he stood there with his hands still on her waist, gazing down at her while the most peculiar grin played across on his face.

"What?" Emily inquired.

John shook his head. *"Nada,"* he said. "It's nothing." But the grin remained in place even as he spoke, and his amber eyes were deeply crinkled at the corners.

"It's something, John. What in the world are you grinning at that way?"

His grip tightened ever so slightly at her waist then when he replied, "I'm grinning at you, my *Emmita.* You're not the slender little creature you were just one week ago."

She rolled her eyes in exasperation. "I'm as fat as a sow. I know. And just as ugly." Her lower lip jutted out now in a full-fledged pout. "How unchivalrous of you to point that out."

"Oh, no, *querida.*" His hands moved to cup her face, and the grin he'd been sporting was replaced by an expression of such earnest warmth that it fairly melted Emily's heart. "A woman can never look ugly when she is brimming with life."

Emily couldn't break her gaze from those incredibly warm eyes. She didn't want to. All of a sudden, instead of feeling like an awkward, overgrown sow, she felt like a swan, all featherlight and full of grace.

"Go," he said. "Before I kiss you." He angled his head toward the door of the saloon.

Suddenly Emily couldn't think of anything in the world she wanted more than for John to kiss her, and she would have said so, but he had already turned her toward the door and given her a gentle push in that direction.

Once inside, it was almost impossible to see. One lone oil lamp burned at a table in the corner. Emily could just make out the shine of Hy Slocum's bald head, bent over a game of Solitaire.

"Hello, Hy," she said brightly. "It's Emily Russell. I'm here to visit your lovely wife."

The man's head came up slowly and he stared at Emily as if he hadn't the vaguest notion who she was.

"Emily Russell," she repeated. "John Bandera's friend. Remember? I was here not too long ago."

"Not long ago."

He spoke the words with a kind of angriness that Emily couldn't fathom. Why would he be angry with her? She wondered if he had expected her to pay for her brief occupation of the room upstairs. Perhaps Sarah could explain.

"I've come to see Sarah. Is she…?"

"Out back," he said, cutting her off as he jerked a thumb over his shoulder toward the back door. "Sarah's out back."

"Oh, good."

Hy returned his attention to his cards then, ignoring Emily altogether.

"Well, I'll just go say hello to her," she said, striving to sound polite in the face of his rude dismissal, walking more quickly than normal toward the saloon's rear door.

But by the time she opened it, Emily was already smiling again, anticipating her reunion with the cheerful redhead.

"Sarah," she called, stepping out into a small patio cluttered with beer kegs and wooden crates. When no one replied, she called again. "Sarah! Hello!"

And then she saw the live oak tree some thirty feet away. There was a freshly painted, dainty little picket fence running around its perimeter, and just distinguishable inside the fence were two white crosses, side by side, one much smaller than the other.

"Sarah," Emily breathed. "Oh, Sarah."

Chapter Fourteen

That night in Santander, John thought he more than lived up to his longtime description of "a man of few words."

Downstairs in the dark saloon, there was nothing to say to Hy Slocum because the man refused comfort of any kind. The loss of his wife and baby seemed to have turned the barkeep inward, where he tended his grief in silence and solitaire.

Upstairs, John didn't know what to say to Emily for fear of disclosing his own heightened concerns for her impending childbirth. *Dios.* It wasn't right for women to die like that, trying to bring a new life into the world. It almost made him promise himself that, if his Emmy made it through her delivery, he'd sleep alone and aching for the rest of his life rather than ever run the risk of losing her again.

So he had divided his time that evening between

Emily's tearful grief upstairs and Hy's stony, silent grief below. At some point John, dead tired, had begun to move his gear into the second room, but one glance at the bloodstained mattress and he knew it was the birthing bed where pretty Sarah and her baby both had died. He closed the door, sighed, and knocked softly on the door of the other room.

Despite the late hour, Emily was sitting in the bed, her knees drawn up within the circle of her arms. Her eyes were dry now, although still red and swollen from her tears. John set his blanket roll and rifle down just inside the door.

"I'll leave these here for the night," he said. "We'll return to the ranch tomorrow whenever you're ready."

"You look so tired, John. Where will you sleep?"

He started to lie, to tell her he'd found a bed elsewhere, but when he opened his mouth to speak, the words wouldn't come. He was so damned tired of lying to this woman. It made his head ache and his heart feel as heavy as lead.

"I don't know," he told her finally. "Maybe in the wagon. It doesn't really matter. It's quiet downstairs. I'll sit there. I'm used to long hours without sleep."

"That may be, but there's no point in doing so tonight." She unlooped her arms, straightened up, then reached over to pat the opposite side of the none-too-wide mattress. "You'll sleep right here."

John shook his head. "No, it wouldn't…"

"Wouldn't what? Wouldn't be right? Is that what you were going to say? Or it wouldn't be seemly?"

"Well…"

"How unseemly can it possibly be, John, now that we're man and wife?" She crossed her arms now over the covers she had drawn up to conceal herself. "And anyway, I do wish you'd stay. I truly don't want to be alone with my melancholy thoughts tonight."

"Then you won't be."

He pulled the door closed behind him.

John had turned out the flame in the lamp while Emily settled herself beneath the covers. She couldn't see him, but she felt the give of the mattress as he lay down and stretched out beside her. The warmth of his body was immediate, despite the fact that there were several inches of mattress, not to mention the bunched sheets and quilts between them.

His mere presence greatly eased her anguish over Sarah's death as well as the nagging worries about her own condition. Somehow it seemed to Emily that nothing bad could happen to her with John Bandera near.

There was proof, after all. Why, even a terrible tornado could pass directly over her, and with John's protection, she could emerge without so much as a scratch. He had rescued her from that bunch of leering cowboys right here in Santander, as well. And, after that, hadn't he saved her from Elliot's dreaded grasp? And there was Lupe's lethal, knife-wielding fit, too. She'd almost forgotten about that.

But the feeling of protection was much more than merely physical. There was a peacefulness in her when she was with this man, a sense of being exactly where she belonged in this world. Funny, she thought, it wasn't so different from the feelings she experienced when she read Price's letters. How odd that a similar quietude settled over her in the presence of someone she barely knew.

Perhaps it was time to get to know this man— this husband of hers!—a bit better. There was no time like the present, she decided, but it would hardly do to begin quizzing the poor man while he was trying to fall asleep, would it? Emily quietly turned on her side, facing the shadow beside her on the bed.

As dark as it was, she could still tell that he was flat on his back atop the covers, with one leg cocked and his arms braced behind his head. Somehow, even though it was dark, she was quite certain that John's eyes were wide-open, staring at the ceiling above the bed.

"Are you asleep?" she whispered as softly as she could, not wanting to wake him if he really was asleep.

"No." His reply was a whisper, too. "But I will be soon."

"You will?"

"Si."

"How do you know that?"

John didn't reply right away, but his silence didn't seem to be an irritated one, for Emily thought she could see his mouth spread just a trifle wider in a grin. When he did speak, there wasn't a hint of irritation or gruffness in his tone. His voice was like soothing Spanish music. It reminded her of a mandolin.

"I know I'll fall asleep very soon because I never get past the *Bs.*"

She blinked in surprise. "Excuse me? Bees? Do you mean honeybees?"

"No, *querida,* I mean the letter *B,*" he said with a tiny chuckle. "It's the little game I play in order to fall asleep."

As soon as John said it, Emily realized she knew exactly what he meant by the little game. It was Price's strategy for overcoming sleeplessness, in which he enumerated living things alphabetically, fairly exhausting himself in the process. He'd written her about it more than once. She'd even tried the technique herself a time or two without success. Rather than put her to sleep, the game kept her wide-awake.

She smiled now, edging up slightly on an elbow, peering down at John, trying to see his face through the darkness. "I know that game. Price must have told you about it, too."

His murmur was neither yes nor no.

"Well, it doesn't work," she muttered, not bothering to disguise her exasperation. "The times I've tried it, I've kept myself awake entire nights, enumerating all the way to blasted Z."

"You tried too hard." John shifted onto his side so they were facing each other. "Put your head down," he commanded softly.

"I'm really not sleepy," she protested.

"Do it."

With a sigh, Emily flopped back down, crossed her arms over her chest, and stared up. "There. My head's down. Now what?"

"Close your eyes."

She did.

"Now watch the backs of your eyelids and see something that begins with the letter *A*."

He waited a moment—quite a long one it seemed to Emily—before he asked, "What do you see?"

"Angels."

In truth, she didn't see anything at all, only darkness, but angels seemed as good a place as any to begin.

"That's good," John murmured. "That's very good. What else do you see?"

Emily concentrated behind her tightly closed eyes, trying hard to play the game properly, but nothing was there. "Apples," she said, trying to summon them up to no avail.

"And?"

"Oh. I see apple pickers."

"Go on," he urged.

"Um." For want of a vision, she searched her brain for yet another word that began with *A*. "Acrobats," she said almost gleefully.

Beside her now, John lifted his head a fraction. "You're seeing all these things? Truly?"

"Well, not exactly," she admitted. "I'm thinking them."

"You're supposed to see, not think, *querida*. You'll never fall asleep that way."

"That's what I *told* you, John. This isn't a game at all. It feels more like work to me." Emily opened her eyes and exhaled loudly in frustration. "Damnably hard work, too, if you really want to know."

"It doesn't work for everyone, I guess." He levered up on an elbow, his shadow looming above her. "So, we'll just have to try something else. Turn over."

"What?"

"Turn on your side. Go on."

Then, when she started rolling toward him, he stopped her. "No, not that way. Turn to your right side so you're facing away from me."

Emily struggled beneath the covers. "This isn't so easy, you know. I'm actually turning two people here, me and the little one."

Once on her side, she reached up to settle the pillow beneath her ear and chin. "There," she said with a sigh.

"Comfortable?" he asked.

"Yes. Quite."

"Good. Now you will be asleep in no time, I promise you."

No sooner were those words out of John's mouth, than Emily felt his hands upon her back as his fingers began to slowly knead the knotted muscles in her shoulders and her neck. She would have gasped in surprise, but instead, she moaned in pure, undiluted pleasure. No one had ever touched her this way. It was firm yet gentle, workmanlike yet intimate, all at the same time. It was completely and indescribably wonderful.

The sensations became more intense when his touch tracked down the length of her spine, slowly kneaded the muscles of her backside, then worked back up to her shoulders and her neck.

She moaned again. "This must be heaven. I really am seeing angels behind my eyelids now."

"Ssh," John whispered. "Don't talk. Don't even think. Just go to sleep."

It wasn't much longer before she was sound asleep. He could tell the difference immediately in the tone of her muscles and their resistance to his hands, in the regular cadence and depth of her breathing. Still, even though he had accomplished his task of putting her to sleep, John didn't stop.

For all the pleasure he was giving Emily, he thought, his own was immeasurably more. How many nights had he dreamed of touching this woman? How many years had he warned himself that such dreams could never come true?

Now, here in the dark, he was learning her body like a blind man, memorizing her like a psalm or a poem. The rhyme of her shoulder blades. The delicate repetition of her ribs. The curve of her hip and the slight thickening of her waist.

It was all he could do to keep his hands from slipping beneath her soft cotton camisole to feel the true warmth and texture of her flesh, to know the weight and wonder of her breasts.

He sighed inaudibly, resisting the pull of sleep in order to prolong this moment, and thinking that all the while he was learning Emily, he was also subtly tutoring her in accepting his touch, making her his wife in more than merely name.

He fell asleep, finally, unwillingly, one hand still curved to her flank, wishing with all his heart that his Emmy could know that her husband was her true and longtime love.

Emily awoke the next morning to bright, hot rays of sunshine pouring through the windows and her bedmate of the night before nowhere to be seen.

It must have been well after ten o'clock, she calculated by the angle of the light. How unlike her to have slept—what?—eleven or twelve hours. Instead of getting up, however, she stretched her arms high above her head and smiled, remembering the night before. It had been wonderful, sheer bliss, falling asleep beneath John's gentle, expert hands.

Her smile widened at the memory as well as at the prospect of similar nights in the future. How absolutely delightful! How shamelessly selfish!

And then her smile increased all the more at the thought of returning the favor with her own hands exploring John's broad shoulders and solid, suntanned back. How shameless could that be? She was his wife, after all, wasn't she?

Just then on the street below she heard a wagon draw up to the front of the saloon and John's voice drifting up to the window as he ordered the horses to stand still. Emily closed her eyes, savoring the sound of him, while anticipating the sight of him when he came through the door of their room.

The next voice she heard wasn't John's, though. It was Hy Slocum's.

"I don't expect to be here next time you're in town, Bandera. I'm selling out, then pulling out. Too many memories here."

"Where will you go?" John asked.

"Dunno. Just head into the wind, I guess. Same as Price McDaniel did."

Emily shot up at the mention of Price's name, but the covers rustled and the bed creaked so much beneath her that she wasn't able to hear all of John's reply. What she did hear sounded muffled, conspiratorial.

"...if you didn't say anything to her under the circumstances."

"Oh, sure," Hy said. "I remember what you said. I won't say one word to her about McDaniel. Fact is, though, I probably won't even see the lady to say goodbye. You give her my regards, will you? And take care, friend. Hope everything works out for you. Better'n it did for me, anyway."

"So long, Hy."

Emily clutched the quilt around her as she struggled out of bed and hastened to the window just in time to see the top of Hy's bald head as he sauntered down the street away from the saloon. It was all she could do not to call out to ask the man exactly what he'd meant about heading into the wind just like Price. Into what wind? When? Whatever did he mean?

Then her gaze shifted back to the man who remained standing beside the wagon. What was John Bandera trying to hide from her? What did he know about Price that he didn't want her to find out?

Anger rushed through Emily like hot steam. She wanted an answer, and she wanted one right now. Leaning farther out the window, she was about to shout down at John, but in that same instant he reached out to smooth a slow, dark hand across the horse's flank.

The big animal shivered beneath his master's gentle touch, and the sight took Emily's breath away. She couldn't have spoken just then, even if she could have recalled what it was that she wanted to say.

They were nearly back to The Crippled B, the horses pulling hard into a stiff and gritty wind, when Emily called out to John from her soft and quilted nest in back.

"I'm sorry I didn't get a chance to say goodbye to Hy Slocum this morning, or to tell him again how sorry I am for his loss."

"I got the impression he didn't want to talk about it," John called over his shoulder.

"Yes. And I got the impression there were other subjects he didn't want to discuss."

John sensed the change in her tone immediately. No longer cheerfully conversational, Emily seemed to be quizzing him now. He kept his eyes trained ahead, on the horses and the road, when he replied.

"Hy's not a big talker."

"That's true," she said. "And neither are you, John Bandera, at least insofar as your missing partner's concerned."

He waited a moment, then told her, "That's probably because I don't care much for speculating."

"Well, indulge me just this once."

Her voice had gone as tart as a crab apple. His Emmy suddenly sounded like a lawman bent on wringing out a confession. "Do me a favor, will you, John? Go ahead and speculate."

"About Price?" he asked innocently, still not looking back at her for fear she'd be able to read his guilty expression.

"Yes, about Price. If my partner simply disappeared, I think I'd have deep concerns, not to mention a notion or two about his disappearance."

"My notions won't do anything to bring him back. I told you, Emily. He's done this before. His roots never went very deep at the ranch."

"That's contrary to everything I know about him," she insisted.

"Well, then, maybe you didn't know him," John shot back, angry at being backed into this particular corner once again.

"Maybe not. I just can't help think that there's something you're not telling me. Something you think I'm not strong enough or courageous enough to handle."

"Nope," he said, hoping the terse response would put an end to the conversation.

"Well, I'd just like to know the truth, John. That's all. It's important. It's more important now than it ever was before."

Eager as he was to be done with the topic, he had to ask. "And why's it so important now?"

She didn't answer right away. In fact, she took so long to respond that John finally glanced over his shoulder to make certain she was all right. The look on her face that greeted him was one he'd never seen before. She was smiling, but at the same time her blue eyes were big and wet with tears. With her golden hair spilling over her shoulders, she looked as beautiful as sudden sunshine through a fine spring rain.

"Emmy?" he asked again, baffled by the disparity of the emotions in her expression, and by her happy tears. "Why now, Emmy? Why is it so important now to know about Price?"

She sniffed and lifted the edge of the quilt to wipe the moisture from her eyes, smiling all the while.

"It's important that I know about Price because I do believe, John, that I'm falling in love with his partner."

Chapter Fifteen

John laughed.

He laughed, damn his suntanned hide! His teeth flashed a brilliant white in the sunlight and his golden eyes glinted as he scraped off his hat, tossed it high in the air and laughed his fool head off.

His reaction was hardly what Emily was expecting after she'd blurted out her newly discovered affection. She was more than a little taken aback by the announcement herself, but there was certainly nothing funny about it, at least as far as she could see.

"I suppose you think it's preposterous, my falling in love, considering we really don't know each other all that well," she said, only too aware of the petulant note in her own voice. She sounded more like a spoiled child than a grown, presumably mature woman whose feelings had been ruffled.

While she pouted, John's laughter diminished to a deep-throated chuckle. Emily watched him through narrowed eyes as he set the brake, then slung his long legs over the driver's seat and climbed into the back of the wagon. With a careful boot, he pushed aside the foothills of her mountainous quilts in order to clear a space for himself beside her. Then he sat and looped an arm about her shoulders, drawing her close despite her initial stiff resistance.

"It's not so preposterous," he said softly. "I'm falling in love with you, too, Emita. What do you think of that?"

"Are you?" she asked almost breathlessly as she drew back her head, the better to see John's face. The expression there appeared to be utterly and amazingly sincere. His smile was frank, even loving, and his warm gaze held hers without wavering, causing Emily's heart to perform a little, ticklish turn. She couldn't help but return that wonderful smile.

"I think perhaps we're very shallow people, basing our affections on so little," she said. "I've never put much credence in the notion of love at first sight."

"We're long past that first sight," he told her.

"Yes, but still, we hardly know each other, John," she insisted. "Certainly not the way…"

His smile evaporated and his handsome face

contorted in a scowl as he cut her off. "The way you and Price know each other?"

She nodded. "Exactly."

"Then, tell me, what do you and Price know of *this?*"

Even as he was posing the question, he was drawing her closer, and *this* turned out to be a kiss that caused Emily to stop thinking entirely in order to abandon herself to the sweet, searing heat of John's lips and the quite unexpected pleasure of his tongue and his teeth.

She didn't want him to stop. Ever. And when his hands moved over her, she didn't want him to stop that either. Her own hands had somehow found their way beneath the fabric of his shirt to discover the slick heat and the perfect contours there.

Desire coursed through her, as if her blood had turned to a river of molten lava, consuming every muscle and bone in its path. Her nerve ends sparked, sizzled and seemed to be going up in flames. It was the most spectacular burning Emily could have imagined, like nothing she had ever felt before.

It was only when the horses snorted and the wagon lurched violently that both of them seemed to come back to their senses. Or John did, anyway, while Emily remained in a warm, sensual haze, not quite able to focus her eyes.

He whistled and called out to the impatient animals, who settled down immediately at the sound of their master's voice.

"Not so smart," he told her ruefully, "making love in a hitched wagon. I apologize, *querida*. I won't lose my head again. I promise."

She traced a bold finger across his lips, still wet from kissing her.

"Don't apologize. I rather liked it, John. Your losing your head, I mean. I hope you'll lose it again."

A brazen little laugh escaped from her throat. "I hope you'll lose it often."

Once they were back at The Crippled B, John carried Emily's luggage upstairs, made certain she was comfortable, and then, without a word of farewell or a glance over his shoulder, beat a quick retreat from both the house and the woman in it.

It had been over an hour since their blazing kiss in the back of the wagon, but John still needed more time to cool off. As he neared the corral, he was half tempted to sling himself out in the water trough, but settled instead for pouring a bucket of water over his head while the little mare, Corazon, ambled to the fence and watched him curiously.

"What are you staring at, *chica?*" he asked her. "Have you never seen how foolishly a man behaves when he's in love?"

John laughed out loud when the mare nodded her head as if she understood perfectly. *Ay yi yi.* He only wished that he understood.

If anyone had told him, during all those long years he spent pining like a schoolboy for the distant and unattainable Miss Emily Russell, that one day she would not only be here and attainable but shamelessly, even brazenly so, he wouldn't have believed it.

It was true, though. She loved him! She said so. And then, somewhere between Santander and the ranch, his Emmy had turned into a she-cat in heat.

There was a sensuous light in her eyes he'd never seen before. They burned blue as flames whenever she looked at him. There was a new and suggestive tilt to her smiles, and a flush on her cheeks that wasn't from sun or wind.

Dios. He should never have kissed her. Not that way, at least. He'd only meant to prove to her that loving a real man was far better than loving some letter-writing phantom.

He'd intended for the kiss to start a small fire glowing deep within her, a pale and dainty candle flame. Instead, it seemed, he'd inadvertently sparked a forest fire, a conflagration that had flared immediately out of his control, not to mention hers.

Leaning against the wood fence rail, he stroked Corazon's soft nose and let her lip the water from his wet hair while he remembered the foal she'd lost a year or so before. Then a vision of the blood-stained bed above the bar in Santander suddenly whirled in his brain.

That wasn't going to happen here. Not as long as he could do anything to prevent it. Not as long as he could *refrain* from doing anything to *cause* it.

They would go no further than kissing, no matter the heat or temptation they felt. That prospect, he knew, would have been less difficult, far easier to tolerate before his Emmy had caught fire.

Eyes closed, mouth taut, John bent his head, pressing his forehead to the mare's long, bony face, thinking just how far it was until the baby came at Christmas. Centuries, at least.

Emily didn't know where John had rushed off to only moments after their return, but she did know how happy and relieved she was to be back at The Crippled B again. Back home.

This truly was her home now, she thought. There would be no more traveling in her future. No steamboats or trains or bouncing wagons. No more packing and unpacking. She was Señora Bandera, and she was home to stay.

John had left her luggage, as always, in Price's room, although Emily doubted she'd be sleeping here again. She took her time unpacking. Every now and then, when she caught a glimpse of herself in the mirror above the dresser, she was startled to see a rosy-cheeked, bright-eyed, happy woman almost winking back at her. She wondered how long it would take her to grow accustomed to feeling so happy and contented. They weren't, after all, emotions she was all that familiar with.

She contemplated her newfound happiness as she lifted a small bundle of letters from her valise and held them tightly against her breast. She knew them by heart, and had thought she knew the man who'd composed them equally as well, but that didn't seem to be the case anymore.

It was John who was the source of her current happiness, not Price. And whether she knew him intimately or not, it was John to whom she owed her gratitude, not to mention her fidelity.

The mere sight of Price's letters now was enough to make Emily feel disloyal. They'd have to go. All of them. It was the right thing to do, she decided. So, with a sigh, she tucked the little bundle in her pocket and started downstairs to the kitchen. If she destroyed a few of her treasured letters each day, perhaps it wouldn't be so sad and painful.

The big iron stove was cold, but it didn't take her more than a minute or two to set a small blaze in its black depths with bits of kindling and matches. Then she knelt in front of the open cast iron door and dropped in the envelopes slowly, one by one, watching each of them flare into flames, then appear to almost dance in an updraft before they collapsed in curls of black ash.

That was how her heart felt, as if it, too, were collapsing in a little heap of ashes. She didn't even realize she was crying until the fire heated the tears that bathed her cheeks. Then, as she was about to let the last letter go, John's soft voice sounded close behind her.

"What are you doing, Emily?"

"Letting go of my past," she replied, dropping the final envelope into the flames.

"You don't have to do that," he said. "Not for my sake, anyway. I'm not a jealous man."

"I know." She brushed the tears from her face and, with his hand on her arm, stood up. "You're a good man, John. And I mean to be a good wife to you. Loyal and honest."

Something flickered in his eyes when she mentioned honesty, but Emily couldn't read the emotion. That was the problem, she thought dismally. She couldn't *read* John the way she had read Price.

"Perhaps you and I should correspond," she said with a little laugh, surprising herself with the sudden notion. It wasn't such a bad idea.

John's dark scowl, however, indicated otherwise. "That's foolish," he said.

"Not necessarily." She couldn't contain the excitement in her voice. They'd correspond, she and

John, just as she and Price had done. Why hadn't she thought of that before? "It's unusual, yes," she said, "but it certainly would be a way of getting to know each other better."

He snorted. "Like a pair of school children rather than husband and wife."

"I only thought…"

John stepped back, cutting her off with harsh words and an ever harsher glare. "Save the letters you already have, Emily, if you need something to read."

"That isn't what I meant at all," she insisted.

"It doesn't matter." He was already halfway out the door when he snarled over his shoulder, "Letters! *Dios!* I don't have time to play such silly games."

Late that night, John walked quietly up the stairs, eyeing the ribbon of light at the sill of his closed bedroom door. He was certain Emily was awake. What he wasn't certain of was whether or not she would even speak to him again after he'd lashed out at her earlier.

She'd caught him off guard with that letter-writing proposition of hers, and he'd turned tail and run rather than confess that the letters she was burning so methodically were his.

After she retreated upstairs, John had spent the better part of the evening at his desk, stewing, scowling while he held a pen in his left hand, attempting to write "Dearest Emmy" even half legibly. More often than not, if the letters were reasonably shaped, he'd smudge them when his hand moved across the page. Realigning the paper didn't help, nor did cocking his wrist at an awkward angle.

It was hopeless, not to mention a worse deceit than the initial one of writing in Price's name. But he didn't know what else to do.

It was too damned late to confess, to risk poisoning the sweet affection Emily had begun to feel for him. So he wrote, crumpled paper, and wrote some more until the floor was invisible under the castaway letters and there was more ink on his fingers and shirt cuff than on the missive he finally managed to finish.

Dearest Emily, it began, *Although I am not accustomed to writing letters…*

He knocked softly on the bedroom door, vaguely wishing Emily would tell him to go away.

"Come in," she called.

John opened the door an inch, sticking the envelope through the crack as a kind of peace offering.

"What's that?" she asked, her voice low and guarded, as well it should have been after his harsh words earlier.

"A letter."

"I thought you were far too busy for such—"

"Emita." He opened the door all the way. She was propped up in his bed, and the look on her pretty face was as guarded as her words, but John could hardly keep his eyes on her face for the jut of her breasts through the thin fabric of her nightdress. For a moment, he almost forgot why he was there.

Ah. The letter. He held it out in her direction. "Would you rather be angry, Emita, or would you rather read this?"

One finely shaped eyebrow went up a fraction, and so did both corners of her mouth. "You wrote me a letter?"

"I did."

Her half smile fully blossomed as she stretched out her hand. "I'm so glad you changed your mind, John. Let me see it. Oh, please."

He hung back, only too aware that the words he'd written were intended to be as awkward as the penmanship, to bear no relation to all those other words he'd composed over the years. These words would never touch her heart. They would simply disappoint her.

"John," she urged, wiggling her fingers for emphasis. "Please let me read it."

Already he could imagine the happy light dying in her eyes as they moved across the page. He could almost feel the weight of the disappointment that would settle in her eager heart. It wouldn't be so different from the way his own heart felt right now, impossibly heavy, aching with deceit.

He crumpled the envelope in his fist.

"Oh, don't," she cried out.

For a moment that seemed more like an eternity, John stood there, staring at the woman he loved more than anything on earth. She was his dream come true, but he persisted in lying to her. She was the mate of his soul, yet he couldn't communicate with her. Words—his true words—whether spoken or written, wouldn't come because they would betray him.

Emily gazed at the ruined paper in his hand while tears trickled down her cheeks. "I only wanted us to know each other better," she said. "If you think I expected poetry, John..."

"I'm not a poet, Emily."

"Yes, I know. And I wasn't anticipating deathless prose, either." She rose up on her knees in the center of the bed, her hands clasped before her, her eyes shining with tears, beseeching him. "The letters were merely a way for us to...to begin. A way for us to touch."

"I'm not Price McDaniel," he told her bluntly while his grip tightened on the twisted envelope. "I don't know how to touch a woman with paper and ink."

"Oh, John." She shook her head sadly as she

sank back down among the covers. "Then I don't know how we'll ever be more than strangers despite the fact that we're man and wife."

It came to him then, as if he'd known it all along, that to touch his beloved, he was going to have to *touch* her. Their union, however long it lasted, would have to be a union of their bodies rather than their souls as long as John was unwilling to confess.

He thought it shouldn't sadden him so. After all, most marriages he'd seen were little more than bedmates carrying out their separate lives by day before returning to each other in the dark. It wasn't what he wanted. It wasn't what he'd dreamed about, but perhaps in the end it was the perfect punishment for his deceit. To have this woman and yet not have her. To give only partly of himself.

"Strangers," he told her softly, "don't feel what we do when they kiss."

Her sad eyes lifted to meet his. There was a hint of blue fire beneath the dull and disappointed gray. "That's true, I suppose."

"No more letters," he said, tearing the envelope into smaller and smaller bits as he walked toward the bed, watching the increasing heat in Emily's eyes and the hint of crimson that began to splash across her cheeks.

The torn paper drifted from his hands onto the

floor like so many snowflakes, and John walked over them, grinding them into the carpet.

Empty-handed now, he reached to turn down the lamp on the nightstand.

Once it was dark, he drew Emily into his embrace, not to tell her of his love, but to show her.

Chapter Sixteen

Emily stood on tiptoe to pin another pillowcase to the line behind the house. The warm September wind, the one that was whipping her skirts around her ankles and threatening to tug all the ribbons from her hair, would dry the bed linens in no time. By noon, she estimated, she'd be upstairs smoothing the fresh, sun-fragrant sheets back on the bed.

Their bed. Hers and John's.

The thought caused one of those tiny, pinwheeling flutters in the pit of her stomach, while it allowed one of those irrepressible grins to take control of her lips. She could feel the color rising in her face.

"I never did see a woman so happy about hanging the gol-durned wash," Minerva Hopkins said, her words muffled by the clothespins lodged in her mouth.

The recent widow had come to The Crippled B

from Kansas several weeks before to visit her brother, Tater Latham, and had agreed to stay on as cook and housekeeper. She had big, capable hands and the disposition of a mud wasp, but Emily was grateful for her help, if not her presence.

"Fact is," Minerva continued, after ferociously shaking the wrinkles out of a damp sheet, "I've never seen a woman in your condition all that happy about anything, Miz Bandera."

"Really?"

"Nope, I never have." Minerva popped the last clothespin from her mouth and jammed it on the taut rope line. "Particularly about keeping on sharing the sheets with her mister. Once a woman gets with child, it's a fact she don't want to have no more to do with her man. Leastways, that's been my experience."

Emily cocked her head at the woman. "You've had a good deal of experience, I suppose, Minerva."

The gray-haired woman gave a snort. "I guess I have. Seven kids. All of them hale and hardy."

"Seven! Oh, my," Emily exclaimed. "This is my first time."

"Won't be your last, either, judging from the way the mister looks at you."

Emily felt that flutter deep inside her again and an increased heat upon her cheeks. Yes, John did look at her with undisguised desire in his beautiful amber eyes, but what Minerva didn't know was that his desire remained just that. Desire. There had been no consummation.

Ever since that night when he'd torn up his letter and turned out the light before slipping into bed beside her, John had been teaching Emily about desire. Teaching her with infinite patience the heights to which her body could soar. Taking her, night after night, with his hands and his mouth, to those stunning pinnacles from which she would spiral down—like spent fireworks—into deep, dreamless contentment.

It had gotten so Emily couldn't wait for night to fall and another passionate encounter to begin. She longed for John in a way she'd never known a human being could long for another. She felt it in every bone and muscle, in every drop of blood in her body. For the first time in her life, she felt complete.

Well, almost complete.

John, for all the heat and passion that he instilled in her, refused the ultimate act of making them one. He didn't want to hurt her, he would say. The baby, he'd protest. It isn't done, he claimed. Too dangerous.

Suddenly Emily realized that she'd been standing there, wind-tossed and preoccupied with thoughts of John and his passion or lack of it, for quite a while, and that Minerva was regarding her rather oddly.

"I'm sorry. I must have been woolgathering, Minerva. Did you just ask me something?"

"Not ask so much as advise," she said, picking up the last sheet and snapping it briskly. "I've heard some of the fellas in the bunkhouse talking about you and the mister and the little one."

"Oh?" Emily stood a bit stiffer. "I don't approve of gossip, Minerva," she admonished the woman even as she was longing to know what had been said about them and secretly hoping Minerva would ignore her stern words.

"Nope. Neither do I." Minerva clipped the sheet to the line, then turned to Emily and said with a shrug, "But a person hears what a person hears, you know. Can't be helped. A person can shut their eyes, but it's downright impossible to shut their ears."

Emily waited a moment to see if Minerva was going to volunteer anything more. When she didn't, Emily snapped, "And just what was it that you heard?"

"Oh, some foolish speculation about how long you and the mister had been married in relation to…" Her gaze dropped to Emily's all-too-obvious belly. "People talk. It don't mean anything."

"It's no one's business but ours," Emily said,

fighting the urge to stomp into the bunkhouse and throttle the first man she laid eyes on there.

"I was in the same fix myself way back when." Minerva moved a little closer and dropped her voice. "I don't often mention this, but I was only seventeen and nearly six months gone when Mr. Hopkins and I said our vows. My young sweetheart had perished in a fall."

The woman's voice was little more than a whisper when she leaned even closer to add, "After the wedding, Mr. Hopkins and I spent plenty of time between the sheets, though, so that by the time the baby came three months later, it seemed like it ought to have been his." Minerva's right eye closed in a slow wink. "Just like you and the mister, I suspect."

Uncomfortable as she was discussing such matters, Emily's curiosity far outweighed her discomfort. For the past three weeks John had been saying that a completion of their union was inadvisable, even dangerous. But now this woman seemed to be telling her not only was it permissible to fully make love at this stage of a pregnancy, but that it was highly recommended, perhaps even necessary for instilling a sense of actual fatherhood.

"You weren't concerned...you and your husband...about any untoward consequences, then?" she asked.

"Consequences?"

Emily cleared her throat. "Any harm to the child as a result of...well...you know."

Minerva shrugged. "We took care, that's all. We took it slow and easy." She bent to pick up the empty wash basket, then stood with it propped against one ample hip. "Don't you worry, Miz Bandera. When's the baby coming? Christmas?"

Emily nodded.

Minerva ticked off months on her sturdy fingers. "September. October. Half of November, I'd say." She winked again. "You and the mister have plenty more time for loving before he needs to remove himself to that room across the hall."

While Emily watched the big woman amble toward the house, she ticked off time on her own fingers. She counted months, then weeks, then nights—at least sixty by her calculations—while a slow smile spread across her lips and that odd flutter repeated itself once again deep inside her.

It was late, and John was washing up in the kitchen after spending most of the evening in the barn, medicating and avoiding the hooves of a rheumy and none too happy stallion.

He worked the soap into a rich lather on his chest and under his arms, hoping to rid himself of the smell of horse and hay, thinking all the while how he'd come to enjoy these soapy evening rituals, preparing himself to share Emily's bed.

Damned if he wasn't turning into a midnight dandy, even to the point of sprinkling himself with a few drops from an old bottle of bay rum that Price had left behind. And if some of the cowhands held their noses in mock disgust when he walked by, it didn't bother him. Emily liked the fragrance just fine.

More often than not, when he was kissing her, she'd make a purring sound deep in her throat. "Mmm. You smell so good," she'd sigh. He would have bathed in vanilla and clover honey if she'd asked him to and suffered the taunts of his men forever, that's how much he wanted to please her.

Of course, pleasing his Emmy these nights wasn't quite the same as pleasing himself. After he'd kissed and touched and teased her to a sweet and shuddering release, and after she'd slipped into a deep sleep, he'd lie awake half the night, listening to her breathe while letting the hot blood cool in his veins and his ragged nerve ends settle back into place.

He sighed and rinsed off the slick, fragrant soap. There were worse things in the world, he decided, than his own pent-up desires. His broken leg had been worse. Well, almost.

But the important thing was that he was binding this woman to him with the pleasure he gave her, and, no matter what it cost him, he intended to bind her tighter and tighter, until they were physically inseparable, until she couldn't fall asleep without his touch.

He dried off, splashed on a few drops of Price's bay rum, adding a drop or two for good measure, then walked quietly upstairs.

"You didn't have to wait up for me," he said, seeing Emily propped against a mound of pillows, a book wedged into the covers over her stomach.

"I didn't have to," she said, closing the book and setting it on the table beside the bed. "I wanted to." She patted the mattress to her left and lifted the covers slightly. "You look tired, John. Come to bed."

Not so tired that he didn't notice the rosy blush on her cheeks or the peculiar slant of her mouth. His Emmy's smiles were usually sweet and innocent. This one, though, struck him as seductive rather than sweet, a come-hither expression if ever he'd seen one.

"Turn out the light," she told him as he neared the bed.

After the room fell into darkness, he sat on the edge of the bed to remove his boots, his habit every night. And as always, after taking off his shirt downstairs in order to wash up, the back he turned to Emily was bare. Tonight, much to his surprise, before he'd even managed to work his foot out of the first boot, warm hands roamed across his shoulders, then traveled up and down the length of his spine.

"Does that feel good?" she murmured, a trace of huskiness in her voice.

Good? It felt exquisite. Her touch lit an immediate fire in his blood.

"*Si,*" he answered cautiously, unwilling to encourage her further, already tempted to the edge by this, her slightest touch.

"And this?" she asked, sliding her palms over his ribs, running her featherlight fingertips across his chest while her lips teased over his shoulder blade.

John drew in a long, measured breath and let it out slowly before he spoke. Even so, his voice sounded winded and shaky, as if he'd just run several rocky miles. Uphill.

"*Cuidado, mi Emita.*"

"What?" she asked.

"I said be careful," he cautioned.

Her hands continued to roam. "Of what?" she asked, her lips vibrating against his spine, her breasts just brushing his skin.

He sighed once more as he tugged off his remaining boot and tossed it blindly toward the wall, then he shifted sideways on the edge of the bed, firmly capturing Emily's wayward hands in both of his.

"Stop," he warned her.

It was too dark to see the expression on her face, but John was sure it must have been one of disappointment, judging from the way her hands suddenly tensed within his grip. There was no mistaking the blend of bewilderment and disappointment in her voice when she finally spoke.

"Don't you want to make love to me, John?"

He drew her close. "More than anything in the world, *querida*," he whispered.

"Then why won't you allow me to give you pleasure, too?"

Her question, voiced huskily, made him chuckle in spite of himself. She was trying to sound sultry and experienced, as if she knew at least a hundred sensuous ways to please him that he'd never even dreamed of himself.

Of course, when he thought about it, that was probably true. He loved her so much that even her offhand smiles and casual glances could quicken his blood. In the past, her words on a page had been enough to raise his temperature a notch or two.

"You do give me pleasure," he said.

"That isn't what I meant."

Her hands pulled free of his to resume their delicate exploration. The pleasure of that touch alone was exquisite in more than a hundred ways. Then her palm settled warmly over his heart.

"Your heart's beating like the great wings of some wild bird," she whispered.

A trapped bird, he thought. A hawk caught in the persistent claws of a hungry cat.

"Make love to me, John," she purred. "And don't tell me it's too risky in my condition, because I know better."

He took one of her hands again, and brought her fingers to his lips. "Emmy, I…"

Outside, somewhere behind the bunkhouse, a rifle shot cracked the stillness of the night.

John reacted instantly, jumping up from the bed and grabbing for his boots. Somewhere in the back of his brain he was aware that the sudden, unexpected gunshot had given him a reprieve and somewhere in the back of his heart he was grateful for it.

"What in the world was that?" Emily asked, rustling the covers as she struggled to sit up. "Who'd fire a gun at this hour?"

"I intend to find out," he said, moving back toward the bed and finding its edge in the darkness. He sat, shoved one foot into a boot, and then the other. "It's probably nothing. Just a drunk cowhand acting up. Don't worry, Emmy. Why don't you go to sleep?"

As he made his way through the darkness to retrieve a shirt from the wardrobe, John could hear her fumbling with the matchbox, breaking two matchsticks and sighing in frustration before she managed to light the lamp beside the bed. When he turned, working the buttons on his shirt, he expected to see Emily cloaked to her chin in sheets and quilts as always. But, instead, the bed covers were tossed back and Emily perched on the edge of the bed, wearing only her thin cotton nightdress.

Even in the low, honey-colored lamplight, he could clearly see the dark thrust of her nipples against the pale fabric and, just below, the sweet, swollen mound of her belly. His knees nearly buckled at the sight. He'd never seen anyone so sensuous, so purely and so exquisitely female. If he'd wanted this woman in the past, those passions paled compared to what he was feeling now.

He had to force his gaze up to her face, where there was no mistaking that his Emmy was still a woman intent on making love. Her blue eyes were as deep as wells and darker than any midnight. They followed his every move like a hungry, insatiable cat.

Dios. He couldn't fight that desire of hers anymore. Not when his own matched it, if not far exceeded it. Not when she looked as desirable as she did. He would have climbed back into bed with her right then, gunfire or not, if there hadn't been a sharp rap on the bedroom door that moment, followed by Tater Latham's anxious appeal.

"Sorry to wake you, boss, but you best come out to the bunkhouse."

"Can it wait till morning, Tater?" John called out.

"Well, it could," the man drawled, "but I don't think it will."

John sighed. "I'll be right there."

He turned toward Emily then, unable to suppress a grin. "You win, Mrs. Bandera," he said as he tucked in his shirttails. "I won't be gone long, and when I get back, *mi Emita,* you're going to have all the loving you can handle for the rest of your life. Think you can wait up for me?"

Her slow, sensuous smile and the glitter in her eyes was enough to let him know she'd wait just as long as it took, and even though they'd been married a month, tonight would be their wedding night at last.

John crossed the dark yard several strides behind Tater, grumbling all the while. Whatever this emergency was, it couldn't be half as important as making love to the beautiful woman currently languishing in his bed.

"What the hell is going on that can't wait till morning, Tater?" he asked.

"You'll see," the man called over his shoulder. "Or maybe I should say you'll see it, but you ain't gonna believe it, boss."

Ahead of them, the lights were burning in the bunkhouse and John could see a fair amount of movement through the uncurtained windows.

He swore at Tater's back. "Which drunken idiot went and got himself shot? Hector?"

"Nobody's shot."

"I heard a rifle," John told him.

"Yep. But nobody got shot." Tater chuckled. "I'd say that was more like a one-gun salute."

If John had been irritated before by having his lovemaking interrupted, Tater's cryptic answers left him gritting his teeth in frustration. They had reached the door of the bunkhouse now, and Tater's hand wrapped around the knob.

"After you, boss," he said, gesturing inside as he opened the door.

"*Gracias,*" John muttered, striding across the threshold, scowling at the men who were gathered around a table in the center of the room. "Anybody want to tell me what's going on here in the middle of the damned night?"

But even before anyone spoke up, John knew.

The man who had fired that one-gun salute was slumped over in a chair, but he managed to lift his chin off his shoulder just long enough to slur, "Hello, John. I bet you thought I was dead."

Price McDaniel had come back.

Chapter Seventeen

A woman waiting to make love, Emily decided, was amazingly similar to a child waiting for Christmas. Her heart wouldn't stop fluttering in her chest. Her lips refused to flatten out, but kept curling up in silly little smiles. There was a kind of heat streaming through her that had nothing to do with the temperature of the room, and a bright anticipation that tingled along every single nerve in her body.

She closed her book with a thump, not even bothering to mark her place, and looked at the clock. John had been gone for half an hour now, but since all seemed quiet out in the bunkhouse, she wasn't particularly concerned. Anyway, whatever was going on that required his presence in the middle of the night, she had every reason to expect that her competent husband would set things right.

Her husband! Emily smiled again. How strange

the way things had all worked out. She didn't doubt for a moment that this physical bond that she and John shared would strengthen, and that perhaps in time they would feel a deeper attachment, one composed of shared feelings and spoken words.

And even if they never had the sort of emotional relationship that she and Price had established, that was something she could live with. All in all, she considered herself the luckiest woman alive to have found such a good and generous man with whom to share her life. Fate had truly blessed her in its own roundabout fashion.

Her smile quirked sideways. Lord knows there were far worse fates than being bedded by a handsome, virile man who set her heart on fire. Her soul, she figured, would probably stay warm enough in the process.

Rather than languish foolishly in the bed, Emily got up and went to the window. Lights still burned bright in the bunkhouse. Whatever was going on?

As if in answer to her question, the door swung open and she caught sight of John's tall and solid form as he emerged. Well, finally, Emily thought. She'd soon be in her lover's arms, and her heart began to pick up speed at the mere idea.

But then, on closer inspection, she saw that John wasn't alone. A lanky man was walking beside him, or more accurately, stumbling along beside him as he tried to match John's lengthy strides. It wasn't Tater, Emily was sure. This person's bearing was far more dandified than Tater or any of the other ranch hands. He wore low-heeled shoes and walked, despite the occasional stumble, as if he were accustomed to sidewalks and carpets, not like a booted and spurred cowboy who was only afoot temporarily.

The stranger wore a low-crowned hat, but even if he hadn't, there was too little light to see his face. He wasn't a stranger to John, though. That much was clear. She could tell from the tilt of both their heads that they were deeply engaged in conversation.

Their voices, hushed as they were, drifted up to the window where she stood. As always, John's melodic Spanish caught her ear. But as she listened more closely, Emily thought she heard a different melody, one as familiar to her as the sound of her own voice.

And then she knew.

Dear Lord, it was Price!

Her heart seemed to move in two directions at once then—flying up on wings of joy as it plummeted in sudden despair. Emily stood there for a moment, unable to move, not knowing whether to laugh or to weep.

Price had come back!

If that was such good, such long-awaited, won-

derful news, she wondered, then why in the world
was she starting to cry?

It was Price's house—half of it, anyway—so
John couldn't very well ask him to sleep in the
bunkhouse. From the instant he had recognized his
long-absent partner, though, John hadn't been
thinking all that clearly.

Mostly, he'd been feeling. The initial shock at
seeing Price had given way almost immediately to
anger, and just as quickly the anger had turned to
fear, and then finally a profound despair.

Price had hardly changed. He was still the
Southern dandy that he'd always been, wearing a
mask of affability that barely concealed his cyni-
cism. His smiles were a little sloppier than they'd
been three years ago and his movements a lot less
than deft. Whiskey still flowed in his veins and
issued forth on his breath while it blurred his vision
and slurred his speech.

The only thing that was different now was that
Price McDaniel was dying. It was obvious from
his ghostly palor, his sunken eyes and cheeks. The
man didn't have to announce it, but he did as they
headed across the yard to the house.

"The Crippled B," he said with a decided snort.
"I guess if a man's going to die, this is as good a
hellhole as any to do it. What do you think, John?"

"It's half yours," John answered tersely, adjusting his stride for his companion's wobbly gait.

"Well, that makes sense. Half a ranch for half a man." Price shrugged, squinting through the darkness toward the house. "I'll be damned if I know why I wanted this cattle-studded, prickly, puny piece of earth. I must've been inordinately drunk."

John merely acknowledged that fact with a soft cluck of his tongue. He could have reminded Price that at the time, back when they were just out of the army, the transplanted Southerner had been hoping The Crippled B would rival any farmland or plantation back in Russell County, but even the thought of Russell County, not to mention the woman who hailed from there, nearly made him sick.

All of his deceptions were about to be exposed. All those miles and miles of tangled webs felt as if they were wound tightly about his chest right now, making it almost impossible to draw a deep, clean breath. They twined in a noose around his neck, choking him.

Losing his Emmy—and he *would* lose her—was no different from losing his life. Price might just as well have fired that homecoming rifle shot right into John's own heart.

When they reached the front porch steps, Price

stumbled and swore fiercely when John caught his arm.

"Your room's the way you left it," John told him, adding, "Nothing's changed much in the house."

He paused for a moment, drawing in the deepest breath he could despite the constriction in his chest. "Except there's a woman…"

Price's lips canted in a leer. "Well, now. I never figured you for more than a one-night man, John. Don't tell me you've gone and lost that fearless heart of yours to some pretty young thing."

His heart felt anything but fearless just then, and John was sorely tempted to confess, one sinner to another, to beg his partner to enter into a conspiracy with him to keep Emily in the dark, if only for a little while longer.

Dios. If he only had time to think, to add a few more threads to the tangled web he'd crafted, to keep Emily and Price apart until…

Suddenly the front door opened, swinging in to frame Emily in yellow lamplight.

"Price?" she asked, hesitant, a little breathless, her gaze fixed on the man at John's side. "Is it really you?"

"Madam," Price said, sweeping off his hat, bowing theatrically. "The honor is mine, I'm sure."

"Price, it's me," she blurted. "Emmy."

"Emmy?"

He repeated her name as if it were foreign to him, which of course it was. John stood silent and immobile, barely breathing, watching the furrows in his Emmy's forehead deepen as she grew more and more confused.

"Emily," she said. "Emily Russell, Price. For heaven's sake! I've come all the way from Mississippi."

"Emily Russell," Price repeated with the slow deliberation of a drunk who was accustomed to being confused and hardly upset by the experience.

But then a tiny light burned through his pale and sunken eyes. "Why, it's Miss Emily of Russell County! And if my mind hasn't failed me altogether, then you must be the little gardenia who wrote me that kind and all-forgiving letter some years back."

Price extended his hand for hers and drew her shaky fingers briefly to his lips.

"My dear Emily," he drawled, "You must think me an awful wretch for never once responding in all these years."

"But, Price, you…"

Her words drifted away like smoke, and then she simply stared at the Southerner while her lips twitched and at least a dozen emotions washed over her features, each one draining a bit more color from her face. John was convinced that she was going to faint so he edged forward, prepared to catch her when her legs finally gave way.

Instead it was Price who suddenly leaned hard against him, then murmured weakly, "So much for happy homecomings, *amigo*. I'd like to go on up to my room now. Will you be so good as to assist me on the staircase, John?"

Emily moved aside to let them pass, and when they did, John asked softly, "Emmy? Will you be all right?"

The sad and bewildered look she gave him in return told him she might never be all right again.

John knocked softly on her door, and entered hesitantly, expecting to be met by the same sad and bewildered expression he'd seen earlier. If that was the case, though, he couldn't tell because Emily was in bed with the covers drawn up over her head.

"Emita?" he whispered.

"Go away, John. Please. I just want to be alone."

Even though her words were muffled by layers of sheets and quilts, her tone was clear enough.

"Don't cry," he said.

"I will if I want to."

"It won't help."

The covers flew back and she sat straight up, glaring at him through soggy lashes. "Well, what else can anybody do when they're losing their best friend in all the world?''

"Price?" he asked rather lamely.

"Well, of course Price," she shot back. "Who else? Why is he doing this to me when we've clearly got so little time left to be together?"

"Doing what?"

Suddenly the blue fire in her eyes seemed to dry her tears. "You heard what he said about my letter, how he denied ever writing me back."

"I heard." John could hear himself swallow. "You didn't believe him, then?"

"Of course I didn't believe him." She sat up even straighter, using a corner of the sheet to wipe the tears from her eyes.

"But why would he lie about something like that?" What he really wanted to know was how Emily had arrived at such an implausible conclusion.

"Because he's trying to protect my feelings. I believe he thinks that my losing him will go easier somehow if we pretend there never was a bond between us."

John almost laughed out loud at the absurdity of it, at her pigheaded desire to keep Saint Price up on his pedestal. At the same time, he was absurdly grateful that her misguided opinion granted him a small reprieve.

"Yeah, well, with Price it's always hard telling

what's truth and what's pure fancy or just plain fabrication," he said. "I guess you intend to play along in his little drama, then?"

She nodded. "You won't tell him, will you, John? I know there's little love lost between the two of you, and I know that Price's arrival has…well…"

Her gaze dropped to the rumpled covers on the bed where they would undoubtedly be making love this very minute if it weren't for Price's untimely return.

"I'll do whatever you want, Emita," he told her. "If it makes it any easier for you, I'll find myself a bed in the bunkhouse for a while."

Tears welled up in her eyes once more. "It's not that I don't love you, John. I do. It's just that I…I'm losing my best friend in all the world."

So was he, John thought. But only for a little while.

Price, in person, wasn't the man Emily had loved so long on the page, but she attributed the difference to the precarious condition of his health as well as his decision to ignore their fond correspondence.

Even after a week, she was willing to overlook his sulks and frequent sneers and to ignore his cynical monologues on almost every subject. Minerva, on the other hand, wasn't willing to overlook a thing.

"I don't care if he is three feet from the grave," the woman said, not bothering to lower her voice even though she was standing just outside Price's bedroom door with a pitcher of fresh water in her hand. "That's no reason to spend every day three sheets to the wind. Especially when it's the drinking that's doing him in."

"Ssh." Emily put a finger to her lips. "He'll hear you."

"I hope he does. Might do him some good. More'n all your sweet talk and pretty smiles." Minerva narrowed her eyes. "You ought to be saving all those for the mister, if you know what I mean, Miz Bandera. He hasn't been looking all that happy lately. Not since His Highness in there hauled his sorry carcass back."

Suddenly something—a book or a boot—thumped hard against the other side of the closed door, and a voice from behind it called out, "Kindly tell that crone to return to her kitchen," only to dissolve into a fearsome fit of coughing.

"There," Emily snapped. "See what you've done?"

She snatched the water pitcher from Minerva's hands, took a deep breath, then opened the door into the dark room.

"Here's some nice, cool water, Price. Why don't you let me pour you a small cupful?"

With the shutters closed, it was difficult to see him where he lay propped in the center of the big walnut bed. But Emily didn't have to see him to know that he was scowling when he answered her.

"Still trying your damnedest to rust my pipes, aren't you? Water's for bathing, Emily, and swimming when one's so inclined."

She heard the distinct sound of a cork popping from a bottle, followed by the slosh of liquid into a tall glass. Sighing, she put the water pitcher down on a table.

"When I find out which one of the cowhands you've bribed to keep bringing you that poison, he'll be seeing the last of The Crippled B and he'll have my footprint on his backside as a souvenir."

"You've gotten rather feisty for a Russell County female, haven't you?" Price took a long, audible sip from his glass. "It must be your close association with that half-breed partner of mine."

"I doubt that," Emily said with a little cluck of her tongue while she bent to pick up the book that Price had flung at the door earlier. "I've always had a mind of my own. You, of all people, ought to know—"

She stopped abruptly, berating herself for once more almost breaking their mutual vow of silence regarding their correspondence. Her occasional lapses only seemed to agitate Price.

"The only thing I know is that I can't die in peace with you and that crone unceasingly pestering me," he snapped. "At least John's had the good manners to make himself scarce."

"He's been working hard," Emily said somewhat defensively, knowing John had made himself scarce from her as well the last few days.

"And he'll be rewarded, too." Price emptied the contents of the bottle into his glass. "Do me a favor, Emily. I'm assuming you won't bring me another bottle, so I'll be most grateful if you'll fetch me some paper and pen and ink. Will you do that?"

"Yes. Of course."

"Good. Then later you can bring that nasty old woman back, and the two of you can witness my last will and testament."

"Your…?" Emily blinked.

Price made a sound that was half wicked laugh, half painful cough, before he managed to say, "What else would I be writing, my dear? Surely you weren't thinking that I was finally going to get around to replying to your treacly little, schoolgirlish letter, were you?"

The sound of his mawkish laughter followed her all the way down the stairs.

Chapter Eighteen

John sat at his desk, trying to focus on his ledger book, trying to make sense of a column of figures that spilled down the page like Chinese characters while the better part of his attention was turned to the assorted sounds in the rest of the house.

Waiting. That's all he did anymore. He waited for the second boot to drop, the blade of the guillotine to fall, the spring in the trap door to give way and send him plunging down. He'd been on tenterhooks ever since Price's return, waiting for the inevitable moment when all of his lies would be uncovered.

And, God forgive him, he'd caught himself wishing once or twice that Price would die, taking the terrible truth with him.

He spent considerable time thinking about the way things might have been with him and Emmy, about what might have happened if he'd confessed to her the day she arrived at The Crippled B. She might have found a way to forgive him back then. If not, at least he'd be able to tell himself he'd acted honorably.

But it was far too late for forgiveness now, and honor, if he'd ever had any, was irretrievable.

So he waited and listened to Minerva's angry footsteps on the stairs, the distant sound of Price's devilish laughter, and finally the soft rustle of Emily's skirts as she came through the door and strode purposefully to his desk.

He closed his ledger, thinking how even the simplest gesture amounted to another prevarication. One look at Emily's pale and tear-streaked face, however, and he dismissed his own self-pity.

"Querida," he said, rising from his chair and circling the desk to take her in his arms. From the way she clung to him, John knew his secret was still safe.

"He's dying, John." Her sobs were muffled against his chest. "He doesn't have very long now."

"I know. I'm sorry, Emita. I know how difficult it is to lose someone who means so much to you."

She pulled back, sniffing, rubbing her wet eyes. "He did. I mean, he does. Oh, I don't know what I mean anymore."

"He doesn't deserve your tears," he said gruffly.

"Seems like all I've been doing is crying these last few days," she said before taking a final, conclusive swipe at her eyes. "Enough of that. With all this blubbering, I almost forgot why I came in here in the first place. Price asked me to bring him paper and pen. May I?"

She was already reaching out for the pen when John caught her wrist.

"Paper and pen? What does he need those for?"

"He wants to write his will before it's too late," she said, blinking up at him. "John, you're hurting me. Let me go. Please."

John hadn't even realized the intensity of his grip. Ashamed, he released Emily's fine-boned wrist, grateful that in his panic he hadn't shattered it.

"I'll see that Price gets what he needs to write his will," he said. "I need to talk to him about some financial matters anyway."

A weary smile passed across her lips. "I'd be so grateful, John. God forgive me, but trying to pretend I'm nothing more than a stranger to that man is just wearing me down."

"You should rest, Emmy. Let Minerva see to Price's needs for a while."

After a mournful little laugh she said, "Minerva's likely to hasten his impending death. They're like two pieces of sandpaper going at each other."

"I'll talk to him."

"He won't listen." She gave a tiny sigh, started for the door, then turned back. "John?"

"Si, Emita?"

"I miss you." Tears welled in her eyes once more. "I've only lately realized how much I depend upon your quiet strength and thorough honesty."

He started toward her, needing to embrace her, but she held up a hand to stop him.

"No, just let me speak. I fear if you touched me now I'd forget what I need to say."

He obeyed her reluctantly.

"I'm not denying that I loved Price's letters or that I'll forever miss his friendship and his poetry. I'll grieve for that loss till the end of my days."

She drew in a long, wavering breath before she continued. "But I want you to know that I'm grateful for the strange fate that brought us together, and to know just how dearly I've come to value...no, to *love* your honesty and your simple, straightforward words."

He found himself staring down at the floor as she spoke, unable to meet that intense, heartfelt gaze that would surely be able to see through his flesh and to read the lies carved on his soul.

"And I want you to know that Price's return hasn't altered my wish to be your wife, John, or my hope that we'll truly come to know each other."

"Emmy," he said, fighting the urge to woo her with the poetry that she longed for, all the pretty words that came so easily when he wrote, but stuck in his throat when he tried to speak them.

Then, as if she assumed he had no more words to offer, pretty or otherwise, she turned again to leave.

"I believe I will rest my eyes for a little while. You won't forget about Price's paper and pen, will you?" she reminded him over her shoulder.

"No, *querida*. I promise you I won't forget."

Price was calling her name, which struck Emily as quite peculiar since he was with her, standing right beside her, in her dream.

It wasn't the real Price, of course. The man who appeared in her dreams was the fantasy she'd created over the years. He was tall, healthy, clear of eye, clean of soul, and sweet to the marrow of his bones. When he spoke, his voice was part poet, part angel. Emily hung on his every word.

Why would he be calling her, she wondered dreamily, when they were already together, strolling arm-in-arm along shady Solomon Street, past the McDaniel place, then somehow, strangely, making their way across a field where scattered mesquite trees and prickly pears poked out of Russell County soil?

"Emily!"

This time Price's shrill call obliterated her dream and brought her, blinking, back to reality. Back to The Crippled B where the man she used to love with all her heart and soul was a dying stranger, and the man she longed to love in that same fashion was barely more than an acquaintance even though they shared such intimacy in bed.

She sat up awkwardly, having forgotten about her baby and her burgeoning shape while she was dreaming.

Price caterwauled once more.

"Yes. All right. I'm coming," Emily muttered, grateful she had fallen asleep in her clothes so she didn't have to bother about getting dressed. It didn't matter if her skirt was wrinkled or her hair was mussed because Price never really looked at her anyway.

She realized as she crossed the hall that she'd slept far longer than she'd intended. Price's room was darker than usual when she entered, making it difficult to distinguish his haggard face from the pillows that surrounded it.

"I had assumed you were taking great pleasure in ignoring me," he said in a tone infused with acid while Emily hastened to light the lamp beside the bed.

"That's unkind, Price." She shook out the match, then replaced the chimney over the flaming wick. "I was napping, and I came as soon as I heard you."

His sallow face took on a sour expression in response.

"It wouldn't hurt you to apologize," Emily said.

"Everything hurts me. I'm dying. Remember?" He lifted his hand and pointed toward the dresser. "There's my will, such as it is. I need your signature as a witness, Emily. The evil witch has already signed it."

She picked up the single sheet of paper, intending only to glance at it, but when she saw the writing—those bold black letters so dominant against the white page—her heart stood quite still and she very nearly forgot how to breathe.

How many times had the sight of that fine penmanship set her heart to beating wildly? How many times had she laughed or cried, sometimes simultaneously, reading the words he'd so carefully etched? How could she do without them?

Forcing the lump from her throat in order to speak, she said, "Your penmanship doesn't seem to have suffered, Price. This must have been difficult to write."

"John provided some assistance," he said.

"I'm not surprised." She was actually reading the paper now, rather than merely focusing on its familiar, separate shapes. "John appears to be the major beneficiary. The only one, as far as I can tell."

"Not that I don't hold you in high esteem, my dear. I just naturally anticipate that anything John has is yours, as well." He coughed roughly, then added, "Besides, my leaving will probably be the best thing I could leave you."

"Oh, Price." Hard as she tried, Emily couldn't keep back the tears. "If you would only..."

"Quit blubbering, woman. I called you in here to put your signature on my will. Nothing more. I'll be grateful if you'll do that and then take your sobs and your moans elsewhere so I can imbibe the last of my whiskey in peace."

"Fine. All right."

Emily snatched up the pen from the dresser, dipped it in the inkwell, and scratched her name at the bottom of the page, only to realize, much to her consternation, that she'd written Emily Russell rather than Bandera. She had to dip the nib once more in order to complete her legal name.

"There," she said after blowing on the page. "That's that. I'll take the pen and ink back to John's desk now."

"Leave them," Price told her.

"Whatever for?"

He was uncorking his bottle when he replied, "Well, you never know. I may suddenly have an overwhelming urge to write a codicil.'' Then he chuckled hoarsely as one bleary, red-rimmed eye closed in a wink. ''Or a letter, my dear Emily. One long overdue.''

After retreating from the sickroom with Price's nasty laughter still ringing in her ears, Emily stepped out on the front porch for a breath of fresh, cleansing air. Since it was late, she was surprised to find Minerva and her brother, Tater Latham, there.

''Evening, ma'am,'' Tater drawled, rising from his chair. ''We were just talking about you, weren't we, Min?''

''Were you?'' Emily sank into the rocker next to Minerva, trying to find the strength, even the will, to smile politely. ''Saying nice things about me, I hope.''

''Nice enough,'' Minerva said. ''We were saying how pleasant it's going to be, having a little one around here.''

Emily leaned her head back and closed her eyes a moment before she replied, ''I confess I've been so preoccupied with dying lately that I haven't thought much about the little one or the future.''

''Doesn't surprise me one little bit. And, if you'll pardon my saying so,'' the housekeeper said, ''that reprobate up there shoulda just gone out someplace and shot himself instead of coming here and causing so much misery.''

Uncharitably, Emily almost wished Price had done just that. If she'd never known the real man, her memories—misguided as they were—wouldn't have been tainted.

"Now, Min,'' her brother cautioned. "McDaniel's got his vices, and plenty of 'em, but he's not the devil incarnate you're forever making him out to be. Why, I can remember...''

Emily rocked forward, suddenly eager to hear something—anything!—good about Price. "Tell me, Tater. Please. Tell me every one of the good things you remember about him.''

He shifted a lean hip onto the porch rail and scratched his head. "Oh, well, let's see now, there was that time a couple years ago up in Kansas when he...''

"It's getting late, Tater.'' John's voice came out of the darkness just before he appeared around a corner of the porch.

"Evening, boss. I was just telling Miz Bandera about the time—''

"I said it's getting late.''

John came up the steps, into the yellow lantern light. It glittered fiercely in his eyes. His features appeared as hard and unyielding as Emily had ever seen them, but the loquacious Tater seemed blissfully unaware.

"As I was saying to Miz Bandera…"

"*Basta!*" John shouted.

The cowhand's mouth snapped shut. His Adam's apple jerked above his collar. For a long moment no one said a word until Minerva rose from her chair.

"Tater Latham, one of these days, the good Lord willing, your ears are going to work half as well as that mouth of yours." She shoved his shoulder. "Go on to bed. Get."

"Yeah. All right, Min." He started for the steps, but not without launching a sidelong glance at John, who was still glowering at him. "Some people just don't appreciate my gift of gab," Tater muttered.

His sister, already on her way inside the house, gave a snort. "Some people just want a little time alone together, you durn fool."

John lowered himself into the chair beside Emily and reached for her hand. It was cold in spite of the lingering warmth of the evening.

"You should go to bed, Emita. There's nothing more you can do for Price."

"He doesn't have much more time," she said sadly. "It was kind of you to help him compose his will, John."

John merely nodded in agreement, thinking that kindness had nothing to do with it. Instead, offering to put his dying partner's final wishes on paper had been his own desperate and deceitful attempt to convince Emily once and for all that it had indeed been Price who'd been writing to her all those years.

Judging from her sad demeanor now, his scheme had apparently succeeded. Now all he needed for his secret to be safe was for Price to die. Soon. Tonight. *Dios.* For his evil wishes, John thought he would probably find himself partnering up with Price again in hell. But he deemed it worth the risk in order to spend his remaining time on earth with his Emmy.

"Odd, isn't it," she continued, rocking idly and staring out into the dark yard while her hand remained tucked in his, "how a person's character can alter so dramatically, and yet his handwriting remains the same? I swear, seeing Price's fine, distinguished hand on that will tonight brought all of his letters rushing back to me."

"Well, at least he did one good thing in his life by sending them to you."

"How can you even say that, John?" Emily tugged her hand from his. "Price deceived me horribly. How can you say that was good?"

"Because," he answered quietly, "it brought you to me, Emita. You and the baby."

"But it was Price I was seeking when I came here. What happened with us was simply... well...accidental."

"*No importa.* It doesn't matter." He reached for her hand again, and held it tighter than before. "It's the ending that matters, *corazon.* Not the beginning," he said, all the while praying for Price's end so that he and Emily and the baby could truly begin.

Die, you worthless bastard. Die tonight, and take my secret to your grave. That's the only way I'm ever going to live.

An hour later, Emily climbed the stairs. Her footsteps were as heavy as her heart.

"It's the ending that matters," John had said in hopes of cheering her. But even though she hadn't told him so, his words had had the opposite effect. She was miserable.

The ending was the ending. Once Price was dead, so too would be all her delights and dearest dreams. Her soul would never again know its perfect home. For all her life, no matter how grateful or content she felt being John Bandera's wife, there would always be a part of her that would be empty, insatiable, vainly longing to be filled.

At the top of the stairs, she paused at Price's door, listening. There was no rustling of covers, no clink of bottle against glass, no labored inhalations. No sounds at all came from the opposite side of the door. The silence was complete, as huge and boundless as heaven itself, as vacant as her soul, and Emily knew without a doubt that Price was dead.

Slowly, taking deep and measured breaths to calm herself, she opened the door and stepped over the threshold.

The lamp beside the bed was burning low, casting its pallid light over the still figure lying in the bed. Price's eyes were closed, almost peacefully so, and the covers were folded neatly across his chest as if he'd known the time had come.

His hands were at his sides. In his left, he held a bottle as if reluctant, even at the very last, to relinquish his lethal pleasures. But it was what Emily saw in his right hand that made her heart squeeze tight.

Emily's fingers trembled when she touched Price's already cool hand. When she eased the folded paper from his limp grasp, she noticed ink stains on his fingertips that hadn't been there earlier.

Before she could bring herself to open the letter, she swayed slightly while she drew in a long breath, knowing the next time she breathed, her life would be different somehow. Better. Worse. She didn't know which. Just different.

She unfolded the paper more slowly than the beating of her heart. Because of the tears in her eyes, at first she couldn't clearly see what Price had written there. Then she blinked hard, once, twice, to bring it into focus, never expecting the penmanship to be small and convoluted, a shaky mixture of print and cursive that slanted awkwardly down the page. Not only was the writing difficult to read, but it was totally, disconcertingly unfamiliar.

With fierce concentration, Emily managed to master the scrawl, her lips silently forming the words as she read them.

My Dearest Emily,
Here, at long last, is your letter. I wish I had responded years ago. It might have saved my prodigal life.

> With my deepest and most
> sincere regrets,
> Price

Suddenly the world itself seemed as scrambled and precariously slanted as those words, and Emily's legs folded beneath her, landing her on the floor beside the bed.

It hadn't been Price. It had never been Price. It all made sense now. It was John who had so perfectly and poetically and maliciously deceived her.

Chapter Nineteen

Still on the front porch, John stared out into the darkness, taking his customary comfort from the late-night sounds of men snoring in the bunkhouse, a breeze pushing softly at the barn door, and the occasional beat of an owl's wings in pursuit of a darting creature below.

The cooling night air promised cooler nights to come. Nights with his chair and Emmy's drawn close to the fireplace, quiet talk drifting between them. Nights side by side in bed, beneath a pile of quilts, whispering, touching. How he longed for their life together, their true married life, to begin.

It would when Price was dead. John was waiting for that. He was keeping watch. He had listened earlier, guiltily, when Emily went upstairs, hoping for the muffled sobs or even a grief-stricken wail that would signal Price's end and his own begin-ning. He had held his breath, in fact, in anticipation. But after the sound of her retreating footsteps, only silence had issued from the house.

Tomorrow, perhaps. The dying had a tendency to will themselves through the night, as if morning somehow meant a new beginning. Then, when first light finally appeared, and with it came no end to pain, they just seemed to expire from the sheer disappointment of it.

He'd killed men, it was true, but always fairly, risking his own life in the process. Never before had he simply wished somebody dead. But then he'd never had a secret to protect or a woman he couldn't bear to lose.

Suddenly John heard the soft swish of Emily's skirts at the door behind him. Her reappearance pleased, but didn't really surprise him. In a house where someone lay so close to death, it often made the living reluctant to sleep or even to close their eyes.

When the screen door squeaked on its hinges, John levered up from his chair in order to greet her.

"Can't you sleep, Emita?" he asked quietly, turning in her direction, smiling as he opened his arms, needing to draw her warm, soft body close to his.

"He's dead," she said.

The door banged shut behind her, startling John, but not half so much as her words or the harsh tone in which she spoke them. She looked as if she'd expended every tear she had, and now her eyes were dry. Dry and hot as a desert.

"It was time," he replied, letting his arms fall to his sides and reverting to his well-practiced, laconic style even though he longed to comfort her, to hold her close and whisper reassurances about endings and beginnings, cold white winters and warm green springs, and most of all enduring love.

The words nearly choked him. The hell with it, he thought. Price was dead. His secret was safe. It was time to begin to speak. But no sooner did he begin than Emily's hand lashed out, hard against his cheek.

"You're despicable," she hissed. "How could you deceive me the way you did? Here." She jammed a piece of paper against his chest. "Read this."

He couldn't. The words were just a crumpled blur at first glance in the lantern light. Then, recognizing the writing as Price's illegible hand, he simply closed his eyes. He didn't need to know what his partner had written to know that his own life was over except for a few, final, furious accusations.

"Why did you do it, John?" she shrieked. "Have you been laughing at me all this while, every time my back was turned? Did you find my confusion and my sorrow so amusing? Was it nothing more than a damned joke to you?''

He shook his head, bereft of the words that had been so plentiful a moment ago, stripped of even the ability to speak.

Emily snatched the paper back. ''For all his failings, at least Price McDaniel never deceived me. He must've thought me an addle-pated, dithering fool, going on and on about our nonexistent correspondence.''

''No, he…''

''And you just stood there, laughing up your sleeve, while I carried on. You were playing with me like some cursed, yellow-eyed cat and me the blind, ignorant mouse.''

''No, *querida*…'' John reached out her, but she batted his hands away.

''Don't you touch me. Don't you ever touch me again, John Bandera.''

He held up his hands in a gesture of submission, and was taking a step back just as Minerva pushed through the door and came grumbling onto the porch. The housekeeper's gray hair was braided for bed, where she undoubtedly had been until a moment ago.

''No disrespect intended, Mister and Miz Bandera, but the two of you are shouting loud enough to wake the dead from here to Mexico.''

She yanked the sash of her woolen horse blanket of a robe, hitching it tighter about her thick middle.

"Salga, mujer," John bellowed, stabbing a finger toward the door. But when the woman stood her ground and stared at him uncomprehendingly, his brain was almost too numb to translate. "Go away."

"Don't you dare, Minerva," Emily immediately countered. "I want you to come upstairs with me and help me pack."

"Pack? Land sakes. If there's packing to do, Miz Bandera, it can wait till a decent hour of the morning."

"No, it can't."

Emily grabbed Minerva's arm, pulling her toward the door.

"When that decent hour of the morning arrives," she said, pitching a dark look at John, "I intend to be as far away from The Crippled B as possible."

Minerva didn't waste any sympathy on hearing that Price was dead. "Good riddance," she said, giving a curt little cluck of her tongue. "I'll do that room from ceiling to floorboard once they haul his pickled carcass out of there."

The sleepy housekeeper wasn't much help with the packing, as it turned out, but then neither was Emily herself. She was still too angry and distraught to accomplish much more than opening drawers and staring blankly at their contents before she slammed them closed again.

Minerva leaned against the bedpost and fiddled with her gray braid while her employer stomped from wardrobe to dresser and back, all the while venting a fury that seemed inexhaustible as she recounted the story of their correspondence from beginning to end, and incident after incident of deliberate deception, certain that Minerva would soon hotly agree that John had used her badly and that leaving was the sensible, the *only* thing to do.

So, Emily was more than a little taken aback when Minerva finally sighed and said, "Well, it beats me why you're taking on this way, Miz Bandera."

"How else would I *take on*, for heaven's sake?" Emily fairly hissed. "Haven't you heard a single thing I've been saying?"

"Yep." Minerva tied a narrow scrap of cotton in a bow at the end of her long braid, inspected her handiwork, then tossed the thick hank over her shoulder. "I've been listening to every durn word. You've been spitting out words like *true love* and *soul mate* and *best friend.*"

"Indeed I have." Emily crossed her arms. "Not to mention liar, scoundrel and craven cad. I'll be glad never to see his deceitful face again."

Minerva shook her head and shrugged. "Well, now, me… I'd feel different about the situation."

"Different?" Emily furrowed her brow. "How?"

"Well, instead of being like you, all hot and bothered and itching to leave, I'd be beside myself with pure happiness."

"Happiness!" Emily exclaimed. "*Happiness!* What in blue blazes is there to be happy about?"

"Plenty, Miz Bandera." Minerva reached for her braid again, inspecting the bow as if she hadn't done so only a moment before. "Why, shoot, ma'am. You just found out that your best friend, your true love, and… what was that other you mentioned?"

"Soul mate," Emily replied softly.

"That's right. Soul mate. I like the sound of that. Not that I ever had one myself, mind you." She gave a rough sigh. "Only men I've ever known weren't even aware I had a soul, let alone wanting to mate with it. You, you've just found out that your soul mate isn't dead after all, and you're mad instead of glad." Minerva shook her head. "I just don't get it."

"But he deceived me. For years. From the very first word he wrote, he made me believe he was Price."

"Well, sure he did. Good Lord, the man's no fool. He knew you wouldn't have written him back a single word if he'd said 'Dear Miz Emily, How'd you like to correspond with a hardworking, handsome fellow who just happens to be half-red Indian?''

''That's not...'' Emily's protest faltered on her tongue. She simply stared at Minerva, who stared back with her lips curved in a satisfied grin.

''If you're not packing tonight, Miz Bandera,'' the woman said, stifling a yawn, ''I'd appreciate getting on back to my bed.''

In spite of the fact that she was looking directly at the housekeeper and watching her lips move, Emily scarcely knew what Minerva was saying right now because she was still hearing the words she'd spoken earlier.

Her head was reeling. It was all true. Everything Minerva said was absolutely true. Without John's deception, she never would have known a love so fine, or a soul so perfectly in tune with hers.

Her soul mate wasn't dead at all, but alive and strong and—miraculously enough!—her husband, who was just downstairs!

John crumpled another page in his fist, then threw it to the floor with its dozen predecessors. *Dios.* His head hammered and his heart had run dry. There were no words left in him except the ones with which Price had warned him years ago.

Southern ladies are just for looking. Touch them and they bruise.

He let the pen fall from his hand. There was no way to say goodbye in any language, no way to undo all the damage he had done, to her, to himself. She would go and...

Emily appeared in the doorway of his office, unannounced by soft footsteps or the swish of her skirts. John looked away. The sight of her hurt too much.

"I'll have Tater drive you to Corpus Christi tomorrow," he said. "Or anywhere you want to go."

"I'm not going anywhere," she said, her silk garments rustling now as she came toward him.

Her voice was strong and level, hardly that of a fragile and bruised creature. Her stride was determined as she came around his desk, kicking aside the crumpled papers in her path. Then she perched on a corner of the desk, idly picking up the pen he had discarded, twirling it with her fingers.

If she meant to stab him, John decided, it would save him the trouble of doing it himself.

"If I went anywhere," she continued, "I'd have to cut out my heart first, John, and even if that were possible, how could I cut out my soul? Why, I wouldn't even know where to find it. Unless—"

Emily stopped speaking so abruptly that John felt forced to look at her to see if she was all right.

She was smiling, but there were tears in her eyes. Or maybe the tears were his. He wasn't sure.

"...unless..." She laughed softly, like a gardenia-scented Southern breeze, and threaded her pale fingers through his while she continued to gaze at him.

"I do believe that's my soul shining in your fine golden eyes, John Bandera. And now that I've truly found it, I'll never let it go."

Epilogue

Natividad Bandera came into the world with a lusty cry on the day after Christmas, 1882, the same date on which his sister had been born ten years earlier. Between the fair-haired child her father had named Alma for soul and the newly arrived, black-haired boy named for the holiday, came Juanito and Russell and Emilio, three strong boys like perfectly spaced stair steps.

The Crippled B had become one of the biggest ranches in Texas, and its owners seemed to be well on their way to making it the most populated, as well. In spite of her slight build, Emily had easy pregnancies and quick, uneventful recoveries. But much to everyone's amazement, the well-bred lady from Mississippi had turned out to be, during labor and delivery, as lusty and loud a screamer as any of her newborn babes.

After Minerva had bathed and swaddled little Nate, and tucked him into bed with his mother, she said, "I 'spose I ought to send Tater out to bring the mister and the young ones back. He bundled them up this morning and was out of here like a jackrabbit the minute you took to bed."

Emily grinned, first at her fine new son, then at her loyal housekeeper. "Yes, have Tater tell him it's safe to come back now. Honestly, Minerva, you'd think after five babies that John would be used to my carrying on, wouldn't you?"

The older woman shook her head. "He never will. For all his size and his savage looks, that man's got a heart as soft as butter. And I warrant it'll be the same with the next child."

"The next!" Emily laughed. "Oh, Lord. Pretty soon we'll have more babies than cattle on The Crippled B."

Minerva had already turned to leave when Emily said, "Aren't you forgetting something?"

The woman stopped, sank a hand into her apron pocket and came up with an envelope. "Seems plumb silly, the two of you writing letters when you're no more'n a few feet apart most of the time. But I know the mister would have my hide if I didn't give you this."

She handed the letter over, then said, "I'll go tell Tater to fetch him now."

"Yes. Tell him to hurry," Emily replied, already sliding the note from its case, greedy as always for the words meant only for her, always for her.

* * * * *

Discover the joys of
nineteenth-century America with
four brand-new Westerns from
Harlequin Historicals.

On sale July 2000

THE BLUSHING BRIDE
by **Judith Stacy**
(California)

and

JAKE'S ANGEL
by **Nicole Foster**
(New Mexico)

On sale August 2000

THE PAPER MARRIAGE
by **Bronwyn Williams**
(North Carolina)

and

PRAIRIE BRIDE
by **Julianne McLean**
(Kansas)

Harlequin Historicals
The way the past *should* have been.

HARLEQUIN®
Makes any time special ™

Visit us at www.eHarlequin.com
HHWEST8

Harlequin® Historical

PRESENTS

THE SIRENS OF THE SEA

The brand-new series from bestselling author

Ruth Langan

Join the spirited Lambert sisters in their
search for adventure—and love!

On sale August 2000
THE SEA WITCH
When dashing Captain Riordan Spencer arrives in
Land's End, Ambrosia Lambert may have
met her perfect match!

On sale January 2001
THE SEA NYMPH
Middle sister Bethany must choose between a
scandalous highwayman and the very proper
Earl of Alsmeeth.

In Summer 2001
Look for youngest sister Darcy's story,
THE SEA SPRITE

Harlequin Historical
The way the past *should* have been!

Three heart-stirring tales are coming down the
aisle toward you in one fabulous collection!

LOVE, HONOR & CHERISH by

SHERRYL WOODS

These were the words that three generations of
Halloran men promised their women. But these vows
made in love are each challenged by the test of time....

LOVE

Jason meets his match when a sassy spitfire turns his
perfectly predictable life upside down!

HONOR

Despite their times of trouble, there still wasn't a dragon
Kevin wouldn't slay to honor and protect his beloved bride!

CHERISH

They'd spent decades apart, but now Brandon had every
intention of rekindling a long-lost love!

"Sherryl Woods is an author who writes with a very special
warmth, wit, charm and intelligence."
—*New York Times* bestselling author
Heather Graham Pozzessere

On sale May 2000 at your favorite retail outlet.

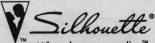

Silhouette®
Where love comes alive™

Take a romp through
Merrie Olde England
with four adventurous tales
from Harlequin Historicals.

In July 2000 look for

MALCOLM'S HONOR
by **Jillian Hart**
(England, 1280s)

LADY OF LYONSBRIDGE
by **Ana Seymour**
(England, 1190s)

In August 2000 look for

THE SEA WITCH
by **Ruth Langan**
(England, 1600s)

PRINCE OF HEARTS
by **Katy Cooper**
(England, 1520s)

Harlequin Historicals
The way the past *should* have been!

HARLEQUIN®
Makes any time special ™

Visit us at www.eHarlequin.com
HHMED13